MONARCH NOTES AND STUDY GUIDES

SHAW'S

SAINT JOAN

by
Grace Horowitz Schwartz
Department of English
Hunter College

Distributed by
MONARCH PRESS, INC.
387 Park Avenue South
New York, N. Y. 10016

TABLE OF CONTENTS

1381589

INTRODUCTION

SHAW'S LIFE: George Bernard Shaw was born in Dublin, Ireland, on July 26, 1856. He lived for ninety-four years and wrote more than fifty plays. He is usually considered to be the greatest writer of plays in the English language since Shakespeare. He also wrote many volumes of literary criticism, art criticism, and music criticism as well as numerous essays on social and political problems; an example of such an essay is the one called "The Crime of Imprisonment."

Shaw's family was part of the Protestant minority in Ireland, not the Roman Catholic majority. Shaw was himself baptized into the Church of England; however, he gave up formal religion early in his life, although he always had a deep interest in questions concerning the meaning and purpose of human life.

The Irish Protestant minority has always tended to regard itself as aristocratic and superior. Shaw's parents certainly felt this way. They were proud of their distant relationship to an Irish nobleman. In reality, however, they led a shabby, disorganized family life. The father was a grain merchant, and his business was always in difficulties; he was good-natured but ineffectual. He found life easier when he kept himself in a state of alcoholic confusion. His wife became an embittered woman who despised her husband and neglected her three children. She was much interested in music; so occupied was she with training her voice and arranging musical scores that she could not spare much time for running her household. George Bernard Shaw and his two sisters were neglected as children. When he was a grown man he recalled vividly how he had spent many childhood days in the kitchen, being looked after by a miserably paid servant girl, and how his meals had almost always consisted of badly stewed beef and stale strong tea.

The one thing he received in his home was a deep knowledge of music and a great love for it. While still a boy he knew many opera scores almost by heart. He could sing a number

of passages from great operas note for note. He wanted to
be a great singer, but he did not have the voice. His voice
was good enough and well trained enough to make him an excellent public speaker in later life, however. Also, he learned
enough about music in his boyhood to give him a foundation
for writing about it; he became a music critic when he was in
his thirties—some feel the best one that ever lived. In an
amusing essay, the first thing he wrote after he got the job,
he explains how his childhood qualified him for the job, although his knowledge of music had nothing to do with his
being hired!

In his neglected boyhood, Shaw received a little Latin in-
struction from an uncle who was a good teacher. But his
main education came from his own independent wanderings
in picture galleries and museums, and from attendance at
concerts, operas, and Shakespeare's plays whenever he got
the chance. Shaw's knowledge of Shakespeare was solid and
detailed.

Shaw was sent to several different schools, always for short
periods of time, and he cordially hated all of them. When he
was fifteen, he left school forever. This boy who was to become
one of the great masters of the English language became an
office boy in a Dublin real-estate office. Here, among other
things, he had the ugly job of collecting rents in slum tene-
ments—an experience he remembered and put to use in his
plays.

At nineteen, he moved to London. There he lived with his
mother, who had left his father and was making her living
by teaching singing. During his early years in London, Bernard
Shaw determined to become a writer. He went about it in a
practical way: he learned to write by writing. Between 1879
and 1883 he wrote five pages every day, eventually completing
five books in this way. Unfortunately, the books were novels,
for which Shaw had little talent. Only one of them has ever
gained any popularity. That is *Cashel Byron's Profession,* a
wildly comic story about a prizefighter. The others were pretty
terrible.

Another important event in Shaw's life took place in 1882. He became converted to socialism. The injustices of industrial society in the nineteenth century, such as the labor of small children in factories and mines, the payment of wages too low for anyone to live on, and the absence of sanitation and decent housing, made a deep impression on Shaw, as they had on Charles Dickens and Elizabeth Barrett Browning. Also, there was a depression in the eighteen eighties, so that Shaw saw plenty of cold, hungry people in London. Shaw was convinced by a lecture given by the economist Henry George, who felt that the inequalities of the economic system could be corrected by land reform. In 1884, Shaw read and was impressed by Karl Marx. However, he fought bitterly with the Marxists afterward. He became convinced that none of them had read Marx. It is interesting that to this day many Marxists are hostile to Shaw. They are stronger enemies to him than conservatives are.

Shaw joined the Fabian Society in 1884. This organization was determined to stop making noble declarations about economic reform and do something about it. This could be accomplished by getting to work on speeches and pamphlets that would convince others and lead to new laws. Shaw worked for many years with this small band of serious intellectuals. The Fabian Society played an important role in the founding of the Labor Party, today one of the two major political parties in Great Britain.

During these years Shaw knew about economic hardships from personal experience. His sleeves were so threadbare that he was afraid to touch it for fear that it would fall apart. But better days were coming. In 1888, he began his brilliant career as a music critic. In 1895, he became drama critic on the London *Saturday Review*. His witty, intelligent, powerfully expressed reviews were so good that it is still a pleasure to read them, even though the actors he wrote of are long dead and many of the plays mentioned are no longer known to most of us.

Through his friend William Archer, a well-known critic, Shaw became interested in the plays of the Norwegian Henrik Ibsen.

Ibsen was causing a revolution in the theater by using plays to discuss and advocate new ideas. This meant that the theater was becoming a place where the audience could find stimulation for their minds, whereas before Ibsen there was nothing more to attract intelligent people to the average play than there is in a historical movie epic of our own day. Soon Shaw was writing his own plays under Ibsen's influence. The first one was *Widowers' Houses*. This was about a subject Shaw knew at first hand—slum landlords. It's merciless attack caused a great furor in the newspapers. It had a run of just two performances in the little experimental theater where it was produced in 1892. England was not yet accustomed to anything stronger than milk and water on the stage. Shaw the dramatist was not exactly famous, but people were certainly starting to hear about him.

Now Shaw began to embody his ideas in comedy. By 1897 he had written *Arms and the Man, The Devil's Disciple,* and *Candida.* He was a rich and famous playwright. In 1898 he gave up his job as drama critic so that he could devote all his time to writing plays. *Caesar and Cleopatra* was written in that year. Also in 1898 he married Charlotte Payne-Townshend, with whom he enjoyed a congenial companionship until her death forty-five years later. By 1915, Shaw was famous the world over. He won the Nobel Prize for literature in 1925, an honor enjoyed by only three other Englishmen—Rudyard Kipling, John Galsworthy, and Winston Churchill.

George Bernard Shaw died in England on November 2, 1950.

SHAW'S PLAYS: Shaw wrote over fifty plays, more than Shakespeare, who wrote thirty-seven, and far more than any other important English playwright. He began his playwriting career in his thirties. His great play about Joan of Arc, *Saint Joan,* was written when he was sixty-seven. In his eighties and nineties he was still producing interesting plays. Like such artists as the sculptor and painter Michelangelo and the opera composer Giuseppe Verdi, he continued to be creative even when he was a very old man.

There were no great playwrights in the nineteenth century

before Shaw. The best writers wrote poetry or novels. There were numerous actors of great skill and there were highly elaborate productions, but all this was wasted on plays that were worthless or on productions of Shakespeare's plays so chopped up and altered that they were hardly recognizable. It is no wonder that Shaw was inspired by Henrik Ibsen. The somber Norwegian had extraordinary dramatic skill, and he used it to treat controversial subjects in such a way that audiences were simultaneously angered and stimulated.

Shaw set out to do the same thing as Ibsen in English, but he soon found out that his own ability was better suited to comedy than to tragic plays. After his first efforts, Shaw wrote comedies almost exclusively.

Shaw's comedy has nothing at all to do with slapstick or non-sense. These are good kinds of comedy, but they are not Shaw's kind. Shaw brings out human foolishness and inconsistency with a bubbling gaiety which is one of his most noticeable qualities. He never ceases to be amused at human behavior, still more at human thought. We may surely conclude that Shaw delights in the innumerable absurd human types, that he loves life and enjoys living it. His writing could not have such vivacity and gusto if this were not so.

Yet Shaw's purpose is in the end like Ibsen's, even if his cast of mind is so different. For him, a play is a place to come to grips with serious ideas, to present new and sometimes startling points of view to the audience. For him, the stage is a place where the dramatist may teach and even preach, and the theater is a school and even a universal church. In portraying a character like Chaplain de Stogumber, for instance, Shaw manages to entertain and indirectly lecture to his audience at the same time.

Shaw's comedies cover a wide range of subjects. This lively-minded, sharp-witted Irishman is interested in almost everything, from socialism to marriage to medicine to religion, right up to and including kindness to animals. (In one of his stage directions, for example, he describes a female character who is wearing a hat "with a dead bird in it." It is hard to imagine a shorter or more effective attack on the practice of killing animals to get their feathers or skins.)

Because of his long interest in socialism, Shaw often deals with money and property in his plays. Shaw is convinced that much evil human behavior is the result of evil economic conditions. *Major Barbara* is the most important of Shaw's plays on this subject. The class system is another frequent target of Shaw's attack. *Pymalion* and *Misalliance* are two plays concerned with this.

Saint Joan is probably the greatest of Bernard Shaw's plays, but it is not his most typical drama. Unlike the bulk of Shaw's successful work, it is not a comedy, though it has highly successful comic elements. The character of Joan does not represent a personality type. Shaw's portrait is exquisitely modeled; it is full of reverence as well as strength. Economic forces and socialist theory do not enter into the play, though there is a remarkably solid discussion of the nature of church and society in the Middle Ages.

A NOTE ON THE ACTORS IN SHAW'S PLAYS: The plays of Bernard Shaw are *stage* plays; they are splendid to read but they are made to be seen. Shaw knows just what will "go" when a play is performed—what dialogue and action will help it to move swiftly and keep the attention of the audience. One of the reasons why Shaw is able to do this is that he wrote many of his plays with definite actors in mind. This kept Shaw's thoughts closely attached to the staging of the play.

Caesar and Cleopatra, for example, was written for Sir Johnston Forbes-Robertson, a famous nineteenth-century actor. Forbes-Robertson's own natural dignity and majestic personality no doubt helped Shaw to some extent in creating Caesar.

What was true of actors was also true of actresses—truer, since Shaw had a habit of falling in love with actresses and writing plays for them as a sign of his affection. (Actresses also had a habit of falling in love with him. This fact has significance, not only gossipy interest. We must remember that the eloquent red-headed reformer and playwright was attractive to some of the most admired women of his day, especially when certain critics claim he does not understand the subject of sex.)

The Man of Destiny and *Captain Brassbound's Conversion* were written with Ellen Terry in mind. *Pygmalion* was Shaw's gift to Mrs. Patrick Campbell. Both were famous and beautiful actresses. The correspondence Shaw exchanged with these two women constitutes two of the most famous sets of love letters in the world. Their wit makes them far more than conventional love letters.

SHAW'S LITERARY STYLE: Literary style is the way a writer has of using his language. It includes such things as choice of words, and the length and shape of sentences. Bernard Shaw's style does not call attention to itself by such devices as elaborate vocabulary or highly rhythmical sentences. The only special quality of the writing is that it mirrors the special quality of Shaw's mind—that is, it is exceptionally clear, lively, and intellectually powerful. It is obviously the result of Shaw's concentration of what he has to say. Language that is fancy or tricky for its own sake is of no interest to him. Students who are reading Shaw's plays are very often studying writing in the same English class. They could not do better than to take his straightforward, vigorous prose as a model.

THE HUNDRED YEARS' WAR

The career of Joan of Arc was an episode in the Hundred Years' War. This was a conflict between England and France lasting from 1337 to 1453. It can more accurately be described as a series of short wars, interrupted by various treaties and truces, over the claims of England to French territories and even the French crown.

CAUSES OF THE WAR: TERRITORIAL DISPUTES: The dispute over English territories in France had its origins when, in 1066, England was conquered by Duke William of Normandy, who is known to history as William the Conquerer. Thus William, the lord of Normandy, a large and powerful part of France, and one of the nobles ruled by the King of France, became also a king in his own right—King of England.

By 1152, less than a century later, William's greatgrandson, Henry II, was not only Duke of Normandy, but also Count of Anjou, and, through his marriage to Eleanor of Aquitaine, Duke of the huge and wealthy French province of Aquitaine. Thus the King of England controlled an enormous piece of French territory. But he was a king in his own right and therefore refused to acknowledge the superiority of the French king over him.

It is true that in the following two centuries or so the English lost a good deal of the above territory through the weakness of their kings, but the uneasy situation remained, and in 1337 the dangerous relationship between the French and English monarchies exploded into open war.

Philip III
(King of France)
1270-85

Philip IV
(King of France)
1285-1314

Charles, Count of Valois

Louis X
(King of France)
1314-1316

Philip V
(King of France)
1316-22

Isabella
married
Edward II
of England

Charles IV
(King of France)
1322-28

Philip VI
(King of France)
1328-50

Edward III
(King of England)
1329-77

Table showing relationship of chief claimants to the French throne in 1328, prior to the start of the Hundred Years' War.

CAUSES OF THE WAR: the English claim to the French crown:
In 1328, the French king, Charles IV, died without an heir.
One claimant to the French throne was Philip, Count of
Valois. He was first cousin to the previous king. Their fathers
were brothers, sons of Philip III (see table). But a sister of
Charles IV, Isabella, had married King Edward II of England
and was the mother of King Edward III of England. Thus,
through his mother, granddaughter of Philip III, daughter of
Philip IV, and sister of the dead Charles IV, Edward III had a
strong claim to the vacant French throne. The French awarded
the crown to Philip, who became Philip VI. Edward was
angered at the decision, but it was not until 1337 that he
made a formal claim to the French crown. At about the same
time Philip VI confiscated all English territories in France.
Soon active hostilities began.

THE PROGRESS OF THE WAR: early English victories to 1360:
In the early years of the war, the invading English armies,
under the command of Edward III and his eldest son, the
Black Prince, achieved two great victories. One was at Crecy
(1346) and the other at Poitiers (1356). In both battles, huge
French armies of mounted knights were defeated by smaller
English armies that included forces of foot soldiers armed
with long bows. The heavily armored knights were so slow
and clumsy that they were helpless against these new weapons.
At Calais, in 1360, the English victory secured a treaty in
which the French completely yielded Aquitaine to English
sovereignty. That is, the English king now held Aquitaine as
his own land, rather than as a Duke under the French king.
In return, Edward gave up his claim to the French throne.

THE PROGRESS OF THE WAR: French victories to 1380: The
strong French king, Charles V (1364-1380), slowly drove back
the English until they lost all their French lands except three
seaport towns. The English did not make a strong attempt to
regain their French territories until the time of Henry V (1413-
1422).

**THE PROGRESS OF THE WAR: the reign of Henry V (1413—
1422).** England's King Henry V has enjoyed the immeasurable

benefit of being glorified by William Shakespeare. He is an important character in the two history plays, *Henry IV, Part I* and *Henry IV, Part II*. There he is shown as the gay Prince Hal, who dissipates his time among low companions until a rebellion in the country brings him to splendid maturity. He helps to defeat the rebels on the battlefield, incidentally saving his father's life. When his father dies, his time for sowing wild oats is ended. He becomes King Henry V, a sober, responsible, and heroic king.

The reign of Henry V is shown by Shakespeare in the play *Henry V*. The emphasis is on Henry's accomplishments in France. The chief events of the play are the heroic English victory at the battle of Agincourt (1415) and Henry's betrothal to the French Princess Catherine (1420).

Historically, Henry V was impressive as a military leader, but he was even more remarkable as a political opportunist. When he came to the throne, England was troubled by intrigues and political disputes. Henry felt that the best solution was to unify the country behind him in a foreign war. Across the English Channel, France was again ripe for conquest. The king, Charles VI, was weak and intermittently insane. His wife, Isabella of Bavaria, had to make many decisions for him. And there was civil war in France as well, for the Duke of Burgundy was in revolt against the French king.

Henry invaded France in 1415. Near the village of Agincourt, the English longbowmen once again cut to pieces a huge French army. After this disaster, the French were unable to stand against Henry. He won battle after battle. In the Treaty of Troyes, the French King (actually Queen Isabella, acting for her helplessly insane husband) disinherited his own son, the Dauphin, and made Henry heir to the French crown. The French king's daughter, Princess Catherine, was given to Henry in marriage.

It is interesting to note that the poor Dauphin thus unceremoniously deprived of his rights appears in two famous plays. He is the boastful prince who sends Henry V a mocking gift of tennis balls (a silly present for a playboy king) and angers Henry into war against the French, in Shakespeare's *Henry V.* He is also the ragged, cowardly Dauphin in Shaw's *Saint Joan.*

But Henry V died at the height of his accomplishments, in 1422.

THE PROGRESS OF THE WAR: the coming of Joan of Arc and the French triumph. A few weeks after the death of Henry V in 1422, King Charles VI of France also died. The Dauphin immediately proclaimed himself king of France, in spite of the terms of the Treaty of Troyes. But the guardians of the infant English king, Henry VI, claimed France for him. They pursued the war once more. They surrounded the city of Orléans in October, 1428. Early in 1429, it seemed as though Orléans would have to surrender.

It was at this point that Joan appeared. A peasant girl in her teens, she managed to get to see the Dauphin and win his confidence. She was sent to Orléans with a small army to try to dislodge the English. A few days after she came to Orléans, the English were forced to leave.

The French army was hugely encouraged by this unexpected victory. Joan gained another triumph at Patay. Then, at Rheims, the Dauphin was crowned as Charles V after the traditional religious ceremony in the cathedral, with Joan present.

However, Joan was captured by the Burgundians in 1430, sold by them to the English, tried as a heretic, and burned at the stake in 1431. She was about nineteen years old at the time.

But though Joan was dead, her work of ridding France of the English did not stop. Charles VII took Paris in 1436 without firing a shot. By 1453, the English had lost all French territory except the seaport of Calais. The English were to keep Calais for another century. English kings continued to call themselves kings of France until 1801, but English power in France was substantially ended in 1453.

It may be added that their defeat in the Hundred Years' War proved a long-range blessing to the English, since it caused them to concentrate on their internal affairs instead of dissipating their energies by meddling in France.

JOAN OF ARC

Joan of Arc (her father's name, from which her last name is taken, was Jacques D'Arc) was born in the village of Domrémy, in Lorraine on the river Meuse, probably about 1412. Her mother taught her religion and various domestic skills such as sewing. She was known in her village as an exceptionally industrious and religious girl. When she was thirteen years old, she heard for the first time one of the "voices" from Heaven which would advise her during the rest of her life. She later identified the saints who spoke to her as Saint Michael, Saint Catherine of Alexandria, and Saint Margaret of Antioch. The voice she heard that first time told her to raise the siege of Orléans.

When Joan told her father that she wanted to go to Orléans to save that city from the English army besieging it, her father, in a rage, threatened to drown her if she ever tried to do such a thing. All the same, in 1429, when she was seventeen, Joan went to the castle of Vaucouleurs and persuaded Robert de Baudricourt, a captain in the Dauphin's forces, to send her to the Dauphin at Chinon. In the court at Chinon, the Dauphin received Joan after some delay. He hid among the gentlemen of the court; however, Joan picked him out of the crowd without hesitation. Joan never would reveal what she said to the Dauphin to persuade him to trust her (Shaw had to invent what happened in the private conversation between them), but she did convince him. After taking the added precaution of having Joan questioned by various church authorities, the Dauphin sent her to Orléans. The theologians, it should be noted, advised the Dauphin to make use of her.

At Orléans, Joan was welcomed by the French commander, Dunois, and by one of the other officers, La Hire. But they counseled her to rest and wait for further reinforcements. Five days later, Joan suddenly sprang up as though inspired, armed herself, and hastened to attack the English. The English capitulated after Joan forced the French to continue fighting stubbornly and outlast the enemy.

A month later (June, 1429), Joan again led the French in a battle against the English and achieved a stunning victory, this time at Patay. Now her reputation was at its height; the French people worshiped her. She came to the ancient city of Rheims with the Dauphin. In the cathedral, the traditional place for the consecrating and crowning of French kings, the Dauphin became King Charles VII (July, 1429). Joan, in magnificent armor, was prominently visible at the ceremony.

This coronation was a masterly piece of strategy on Joan's part. The Dauphin had been disinherited in favor of the English king by the Treaty of Troyes in 1420. (See section on the Hundred Years' War, above). His own mother had cast doubts on his legitimacy. Now all this did not matter. Charles was properly crowned at Rheims; to the French people this meant that he was their rightful king.

Joan's next goal was the capture of Paris. The King and his counselors were not willing to follow her daring plans. Well contented with his achievements, Charles disbanded his army and sent most of his soldiers home.

Joan returned to active campaigning in March of 1430, when the rebel Burgundians threatened the city of Compiègne. Swiftly she left Charles to his aimless procession from one castle to another, after having followed him discontentedly over the countryside for months. With a small force, she set out to rescue Compiègne.

During the battle, the English managed to outflank the French troops. Joan stayed behind to the last in order to protect the rear as the French retreated. While doing this, she was taken prisoner by the Burgundians.

As soon as the news of Joan's capture reached the English, they tried to get her from the Burgundians. Her legend was such a potent force against them that they were determined

that she would die. The Burgundians hesitated and vacillated,
but at last, in January, 1431, Joan was in English hands.

Rather than dispose of her directly, the English turned her
over to a church court for trial. Her judges were Pierre
Cauchon, Bishop of Beauvais, a prominent sympathizer with
the English and Burgundians (Shaw uses Peter, the English
version of his first name), and Jean La Maistre, the Vice-
Inquisitor of France. Thus, in January, 1431, there began at
the city of Rouen a detailed examination and trial of Joan
which lasted for five months, until her death at the end of
May. The questioning of Joan was lengthy and frequent; she
was exhausted by the strain of it. Her imprisonment, too, was
hard on her, for she was a country girl, used to freedom and
the outdoors. But she was never questioned under torture,
which was usual in such a case.

The charges against her, originally seventy in number, were
reduced to twelve before the trial itself took place. She was
charged with wearing men's clothing, and with stating that
the saints spoke to her in French rather than in English. But
the most serious charges were those of presumptuousness,
blasphemy, and heresy. Joan, it was charged, refused to sub-
mit herself to the wisdom of the Church; when the Church
told her that her voices were not from God, she insisted that
they were. She believed that she was in direct communication
with Heaven, without the intervention of the Church. She
dared to speak in the name of Jesus and Mary.

Her judges urged her repeatedly to repent and give up her
sinful behavior. Cauchon himself went so far as to visit her in
prison and try to persuade her personally. But she stood stead-
fast until her condemnation was prepared and she was about
to be handed over to the "secular arm" (in this case, the
English) for execution. Then, overcome by terror, she signed
a document admitting her former errors and repenting. There-
upon she was sentenced to life imprisonment rather than to
death.

A few days later, Joan put on men's clothes once more. She
cried that her voices were angry at her for what she had

done. They called her admission of sin treason. She took it back and once more insisted that her voices were sent by God. (In the play, Shaw telescopes these events into a shorter time; Joan admits error, is horrified to find herself sentenced to perpetual captivity, and immediately tears up her confession.)

At last, the English were able to carry out their long-hoped-for destruction of Joan. She was burned alive as a heretic, a rebel against the doctrines of the Catholic Church. But first Cauchon permitted her to make her confession and receive holy communion, a really extraordinary privilege for a condemned heretic. As she was dying, with her last breath she called to Jesus. The executioner of Rouen testified later that her heart would not burn.

In 1450, Charles VII called an inquiry into Joan's trial. The rehabilitation of Joan's memory was valuable to him politically; to have been crowned at Rheims by a maid sent from God was far preferable to owing his coronation to an accursed heretic. Even so, Charles waited twenty years to take this step; and there is no record that he made the slightest effort to save Joan while she was alive.

Joan's memory was cleared of all accusations in 1456. She was made a saint in 1920. Her canonization (elevation to sainthood) inspired Bernard Shaw to write his play.

JOAN OF ARC IN LITERATURE

Bernard Shaw himself offers a survey of those works on Joan of Arc written before his own play. (See the Preface to *Saint Joan*, the section entitled "The Maid in Literature.") He mentions prominently the writings of Voltaire, Anatole France, Andrew Lang, and Mark Twain.

It is also proper to note that Shaw's play is not the last word to be spoken on the subject of the young warrior-saint. *Saint Joan* is such a great achievement that it has come to command almost universal respect. Yet in some ways it is distinctly unorthodox in viewpoint—for instance, in its praise of Cauchon and the Inquisitor, and in Shaw's unwillingness to accept Joan's voices as the actual voices of saints. Two recent treatments of Joan's story in dramatic form are Maxwell Anderson's *Joan of Lorraine* and Jean Anouilh's *The Lark*. Though they probably are as good as *Saint Joan*, they are of interest because they provide different viewpoints from that of Shaw. The student might well read them in conjunction with *Saint Joan* to get a well-rounded understanding of the subject.

THE PLAY IN PRODUCTION

Saint Joan was first produced by the Theatre Guild in New York City, in 1923. The leading role was played by Winifred Lenihan, an actress who, in the opinion of most critics, has never been surpassed in the part. Shortly after, the London production starred Sybil Thorndike; she also scored a great success. She was seen later in numerous revivals of the play.

Both in England and America, the play was an instant success with critics and public. There was general amazement that such an elderly man as Shaw (he was sixty-seven in 1923) could produce so striking a work. It gained the reputation of the greatest play in English since the death of Shakespeare, and it has retained that high position since.

The play has been enduringly popular. There have been constant revivals. In recent times, the Irish actress Siobhan McKenna has had much praise in the role. An ambitious film version of the play, produced by Otto Preminger, has been unfavorably received.

DETAILED COMMENTARY

THE PREFACE

GENERAL COMMENT: Bernard Shaw's Preface to *Saint Joan* is a long, substantial essay, challenging in content and vigorous in style. It is touched with flashes of wit, but on the whole it is serious and carefully reasoned. The essay is divided into forty-one separate sections, in which Shaw discusses such matters as Joan's mind and character, her life, her weaknesses, her relationship with the great institutions of her time, modern views of Joan, and the play *Saint Joan* itself.

Shaw cannot accept the religious view of Joan as one who was actually advised by the voices of saints and eventually driven to her death by a villainous bishop. Nor can he accept the other, disillusioned idea of Joan as an unbalanced village girl suffering from hallucinations. Instead, he sees Joan as a genius—one whose natural capabilities are of a completely different order from those of ordinary people. Shaw explains that Joan was what the great British scientist Francis Galton called a visualizer—a person whose energy and imagination were so great that she formulated her ideas as voices speaking to her. Many other great geniuses, such as Martin Luther, had similarly dramatic imaginations. The form of these ideas does not affect their brilliance.

Thus, though Shaw cannot accept any organized religious faith, and though to him Joan cannot be accepted as a person miraculously directed by divine voices, she is nevertheless amazing in another way. She is one of those people who appear at very rare intervals among humanity, to give to the rest of us some idea of the endless potential of man. She is an example of the possibility of human development. As such, she is miraculous. Therefore, Shaw ends in an attitude of deep reverence toward Joan. The most pious historian could not respect her more. The Preface, in which Shaw formulates these ideas, will be briefly summarized, one section at a time. Each section will be discussed as necessary. In this way, we may hope to grasp Shaw's many-sided view of Saint Joan. The Preface undoubtedly requires more than a single reading from a student. Perhaps the best method is to read it carefully before reading the play and again afterward.

JOAN THE ORIGINAL AND PRESUMPTUOUS: Joan of Arc was born in 1412, burned at the stake in 1431, and rehabilitated in 1456. In the twentieth century, the Church took the successive steps necessary to make her a saint: she was declared "venerable" in 1904, called "blessed" in 1908, and elevated to sainthood in 1920.

In spite of this, Joan was a Protestant in spirit; also, she was a nationalist in her political thinking and a realist in military strategy. In addition, she was a pioneer of sensible clothes for women.

COMMENT: Shaw here expresses the contradictory concepts which are at the heart of his portrait of Joan. He states that Joan was executed because she represented ideas that were far ahead of her time. She was a devoted daughter of the Roman Catholic Church, and, in fact, eventually became a saint of that Church. But she was a Protestant, though she did not know it. By this, Shaw means the following: she felt that her relationship with God was a direct one; she would not accept the Church as intermediary between God and herself. When there was a conflict between what the Church told her and what she felt Heaven was telling her, she would listen only to Heaven. This reliance on the individual conscience rather than on an organized religious institution later came to be essential to Protestant religious thought.

When Shaw calls Joan a nationalist, he is referring to her consciousness of the unity of French-speaking people. In the feudal system, which was the social and political organization of the Middle Ages, a man's loyalty was to his lord. Society was organized into a pyramid of classes; every man had his master and his inferior (except the serfs (the poorest farmers), who had no inferiors. A man's loyalty was to his own class, and his duty belonged to the class above him. Thus, to be a knight in the Middle Ages had much meaning. But to be a Frenchman did not have much meaning.

Unlike most of her countrymen, Joan was deeply conscious of being French. To her, the war was a holy war to drive the English from French soil. The French land belonged to the French people. Joan succeeded in inspiring the French soliders with this feeling. They felt that they had a personal, emotional reason for fighting. As a result, they were far more dangerous and effective as soldiers.

This in part is what Shaw refers to when he calls Joan a realist in warfare. In the Middle Ages, battles were sometimes little more than ceremonious tournaments, in which gentlemenly contestants competed to see who would be a prisoner and who would collect ransom. (The lowly foot soldiers, however, always found war a dirty business.) But Joan fought for the sake of France. She believed that it was God's will that she drive the English from French soil. Therefore, she put her life in God's hands, and her soldiers learned to do the same. She fought to win; she willingly risked her life to obtain victory.

Joan accomplished all of the above with great force and little concern for the feelings of others. She gave orders to kings and churchmen in God's name. She won battles by ignoring the plans of generals. Shaw points out that she was really burned for her tactlessness and presumption.

JOAN AND SOCRATES: Joan knew nothing of flattering and managing men. She corrected their mistakes openly and was surprised that they were not grateful. She did not realize how people hate anyone who exposes their stupidities. Socrates was the same. When put on trial for his life, he did not understand that he really was being tried for showing up the foolishness of ordinary men.

COMMENT: Socrates was a very famous Greek philosopher, known for his moral principles as well as his great intelligence. He wrote nothing himself; we know of him mainly through the writings of Plato. He was tried and executed in 399 B. C. for corrupting the minds of the young. Shaw points out that he was really killed for making the majority of people uncomfortably conscious that they were stupid.

CONTRAST WITH NAPOLEON: Napoleon, like Socrates and Joan, had enormous ability, but he did not have their benevolence. Like them, he was hated, but he knew it. He at least died in his bed, though in captivity on the island of St. Helena. This shows that it is safer to be a conqueror than a saint.

COMMENT: Napoleon Bonaparte was the French soldier who rose to prominence as general and emperior of France in the early nineteenth century, after the French Revolution. He suffered defeat at the battle of Waterloo in 1815, at the hands of the Duke of Wellington. He was imprisoned on the little island of St. Helena, where he died.

"Herod and Pilate, . . . Annas and Caiaphas" are used as symbols of legal authority. Herod Antipas was Prince of Judea, and Pontius Pilate was Roman governor of Judea; both played a part in the condemnation of Christ. Annas and Caiaphas were high priests in Jerusalem, Annas being the one before whom St. Paul was brought to trial. Shaw's point is that miraculously good people like Christ and Joan are killed because they are mysterious and therefore frightening. But ordinary government officials are understandable; thus they die in their beds, even when they are scoundrels.

WAS JOAN INNOCENT OR GUILTY: Joan's trial was honest and conscientious, far more so than any controversial prisoner would get today. The investigation of 1456 which rehabilitated her, as well as her canonization, have shown, nevertheless, that she was innocent of the charges of witchcraft, harlotry, blasphemy, and idolatry. Her one real crime was her great presumption, a result of her genius.

COMMENT: Here Shaw brings out another contradiction
or paradox, as it is usually called. Joan's trial was fair and
her condemnation reasonable, by the standards of the
time and circumstances. Yet the trial failed to take into
account the one central, all-important fact—Joan was a
genius and a saint.

A genius, Shaw states, is a person with a set of values
different from that of most people, because he possesses
far greater understanding than they do. A saint is a person
showing extraordinary virtues and supernatural powers,
according to the definition of the Church. Clearly, to
Shaw, the two, genius and saint, nearly coincide. Furthermore, Joan's genius was of a practical type—military and
political. Many historians feel that women are not supposed to excel in these areas. This gives them an unconscious prejudice that warps their judgment of Joan. Thus
they do not really understand her and make her into a
pretty, helpless romantic heroine.

Here Shaw brings into the discussion one of his most
characteristic ideas, that of the genius or, as Shaw sometimes names him, the Superman. The genius or Superman
is an accident of heredity. He is that highly unusual person who shows qualities of a far superior type to the
normal ones. His abilities, that is, are not just greater
than most people's, but are of an entirely different order.
As the human race strives and develops, Shaw feels, one
day all people may have the qualities of the Superman.
In fact, Shaw is convinced that the process of evolution
is being directed toward that purpose by what Shaw calls
the Life Force. This Life Force which wants to make a
better humanity is a central creative impulse, not exactly
like the God of the Bible, but very closely related to God
nonetheless.

Shaw discusses the idea of the Superman and the Life
Force in his play *Man and Superman*. Caesar in Shaw's
play *Caesar and Cleopatra* is also a genius or Superman.

We also see in this section of the Preface Shaw's aggres-

sive feminism. He points out that a woman is simply a
female human being, and not a strange animal. There is
no particular reason, Shaw points out, why a woman
should not be gifted at soldiering or politics.

JOAN'S GOOD LOOKS: There is no evidence that Joan was
pretty or sexually attractive. This does not mean she was ugly
but only that she was entirely uninterested in the sexual pur-
suit of the male. She had other things to do.

COMMENT: Shaw is developing further the idea that
Joan of Arc was not a conventional romantic heroine.

JOAN'S SOCIAL POSITION: Joan was the daughter of a
farmer. Her family was not rich, but it was far from poor.
She worked on the farm, tending sheep and taking care of the
household, but she was not a drudge. Her father was an important man in village affairs in her native Domrémy. Joan
herself knew much about politics and the progress of the war,
even though she could neither read nor write.

COMMENT: Shaw is battling against the tendency to
view Joan as virtually a beggar maid. He points out wit-
tily that romantic-minded people like their heroines to
be either beggars or princesses. Joan's family was in fact
middle class, and Joan herself was well trained and aware
of the world about her. The fact that she was illiterate
was not of great importance, either for her or those who
came into contact with her. The ability to read and write
was not common then, as it is today.

JOAN'S VOICES AND VISIONS: What is the explanation for
Joan's voices and visions? Was she mad? Was she a saint? The
voices prove none of this. Joan simply received her own in-
tuitions in this particularly vivid way. Other geniuses have
had similarly powerful imaginative faculties. Examples are
the Greek philosopher Socrates, the religious leader Martin
Luther, the philosopher Emanuel Swedenborg, and the English poet, artist, and mystic William Blake.

COMMENT: The test of Joan's ideas is not how they came

to her, but how sensible they were. Shaw shows that all
of them were perfectly reasonable and logical. For instance, it was good sense to wear a soldier's clothing when
she lived among soldiers. If she were dressed as a woman,
she could not have stayed with the army safely and without reference to sex.

Joan's rescue of the city of Orléans, followed by the Dauphin's coronation, show the practical genius of a Napoleon. That Joan was sure Saint Catherine and Saint
Margaret told her to do these things does not alter their
brilliance.

In other words, Shaw rejects the supernatural origin of
Joan's ideas. Yet he finds that they were still miraculous,
in the sense that they came from her extraordinary intui-
tive understanding and vivid imagination—qualities beyond those most human beings possess.

THE EVOLUTIONARY APPETITE: Joan certainly was not a
mental defective who suffered from delusions. On the other
hand, Shaw cannot accept the theory that three saints did
actually appear to Joan with instructions from God, though
this second explanation is far nearer the truth than the first.
Joan was an instrument of a great force. Shaw calls it the
evolutionary appetite.

COMMENT: Shaw often discusses the idea of the evolutionary appetite. Usually, he calls it the Life Force. It is
that powerful impulse which sends certain human beings
on a hunt for human betterment, even though they will
not themselves profit in any way from this, and even
though they may suffer great personal hardship as a
result of their efforts.

Shaw believes that Life is constantly trying to improve
itself. Life has used and discarded many creatures in this
effort (the dinosaur, for instance) and with the same
ruthlessness, it will seize hold of a helpless human being
and make him (or her) its instrument in this huge struggle. Joan was such an instrument.

THE MERE ICONOGRAPHY DOES NOT MATTER: In different
religions, the hopes and searchings of man are given different
forms. Usually there is a figure who represents an Almighty
Father. Visionaries see such embodiments, where most of us
just think about them.

COMMENT: Shaw means that the difference between
religions is mainly a difference in the symbolic representation of human conscience. That is, man invents a Father-
like deity to represent his own deepest sense of what is
good. Thus, Shaw can understand and appreciate Joan,
though he himself has not been brought up amid Roman
Catholic symbols.

THE MODERN EDUCATION WHICH JOAN ESCAPED: Today,
modern science has nothing but contempt for Joan's visions.
The scientists substitute the worship of Louis Pasteur for
the worship of the saints. Joan worshiped the symbols of the
spirit. We worship soulless quackery.

COMMENT: Shaw here attacks modern scientific thought.
The attack has only the vaguest connection with the
subject of Joan and her voices. Shaw singles out the
French physiologist Paul Bert (1833-1886) and especially
the great scientist Louis Pasteur (1822-1895), whose in-
vestigations established the germ theory and made a monu-
mental contribution to the control of disease. One dis-
covery of Pasteur was that if weak disease cultures were
injected into a living creature, that creature would build
up a resistance to powerful cultures of the same disease.
Thus the principle of immunization was discovered, giving
man eventual mastery over such terrible diseases as diph-
theria and polio.

Shaw was disgusted by the idea of injecting diseased
matter into human beings. He was a fanatical enemy of
vaccines of all kinds. This is one area of Shaw's thought
where his independence turns into the eccentricity of the
crank; most critics agree on this. Shaw did not fully
understand the scientific thought of his time; he had an
almost superstitious mistrust of it. This is a sad example

of the enmity between literature and science which we hear so much about today.

FAILURES OF THE VOICES: Joan's voices assured her that she would be rescued during her trial. This shows that the voices were simply extensions of her own thoughts. She knew that a friendly army was nearby. She did not realize that her friends were as glad to be rid of her as her enemies. Nor did she understand how serious it would have been to take her by force from the hands of the Church. It seemed reasonable to her that she would be rescued. Therefore, Saint Catherine told her that this was so.

> **COMMENT:** Shaw uses the theory that Joan's voices were the formulations of her own mind to explain her behavior at the trial. The voices of the saints told her she would be saved. This reflects Joan's own erroneous belief. When she was not saved, she recanted and threw herself at the feet of the Church, with the sensible purpose of avoiding death. However, after she found that she would be a prisoner for life, she took back her confession of error. Again, she said her voices told her to.

> Shaw's explanation of Joan of Arc's conduct is reasonable and may be quite correct. However, we must remember that her withdrawal of her confession did not come immediately after her sentence to life imprisonment. In real life, several days elapsed between the two. Thus, cause and effect are not as obvious as Shaw makes them.

JOAN'S MANLINESS AND MILITARISM: In Joan's childhood, she already wanted to live the life of a soldier. At the court of France after her victories, when she could easily have resumed woman's dress, she continued to dress as a soldier. She was by nature one of those "unwomanly women" who prefer to live a man's life.

> **COMMENT:** We must note carefully that when Shaw talks of Joan in this way, he makes no suggestion of sexual abnormality. In earlier sections, he points out that Joan never gave up the possibility that she might some day

marry. Her capacities were such that leading the limited existence available to women did not appeal to her.

Rosa Bonheur (1882-1899) was a French painter who specialized in the painting of animals. She dressed like a man in order to avoid notice when she visited markets and fairs to study animals.

George Sand was the pen name of Aurore Dupin (1804-1876); she was a famous French novelist who occasionally wore masculine clothing. The writer Alfred de Musset and the composer Frédéric Chopin were among her lovers.

Bernard Shaw uses the above two women as examples of other famous women besides Joan of Arc for whom the life of a man had some appeal.

WAS JOAN SUICIDAL: Joan did risk her life in battle. She also jumped from a tower in an effort to escape from prison. But she was not suicidal.

JOAN SUMMED UP: Joan was a girl of exceptional capability and sanity.

COMMENT: Here we find a listing of those qualities that Shaw has been discussing in the previous sections of this Preface. He mentions Joan's military ability: she knew how to use artillery and understood how to hang on doggedly until the enemy gave in. Shaw sees Joan as a peasant who showed her sensible, respectable country origins. She hated bad language and insisted on proper religious observances.

Joan was able to deal with people of all social classes. By one means or another, she usually managed to get them to do what she wanted.

This section is a general appreciation of Joan as a human being, rather than as a genius-saint.

JOAN'S IMMATURITY AND IGNORANCE: We must also remember that Joan was a girl in her teens. Because of her youth she lacked tact. Because of her ignorance, she did not understand the great institutions of her own time, feudalism and Catholicism.

COMMENT: In an attempt to explain Joan's failures as well as her successes, Shaw enumerates her great weaknesses—innocence and ignorance. He stresses again her awkwardness in human relations: she wrote to kings and ordered them to change their governments. She was unable to understand why such actions caused resentment. We find also a brief statement that Shaw will develop elaborately in the play itself. When Joan glorified France as a nation she was unknowingly setting herself up against the feudal system and the Catholic Church, both of which were international. (See Comment on the first section of this Preface, above.)

THE MAID IN LITERATURE: Joan's legend has been dealt with by numerous important writers. These treatments have usually been either scurrilous attacks or over-romantic tributes. Among the attackers have been Shakespeare in the first part of *King Henry VI*, Voltaire in *La Pucelle,* and Anatole France in his biography of Joan. Those who wrote adoring romantic tributes to Joan have included Schiller, Andrew Lang, and Mark Twain.

COMMENT: Shaw includes a number of literary references here in an extremely compressed form. Below they are identified.

WILLIAM SHAKESPEARE: The great English dramatist wrote a three-part history of *King Henry VI* during the early years of his career. (It is quite possible, as Shaw indicates, that Shakespeare did not write the plays in their entirety, but simply revised some earlier plays written by somebody else.) In Part I of *King Henry VI*, Joan of Arc is one of the characters. She is depicted from a hostile English viewpoint as a witch and an immoral woman.

VOLTAIRE (1694-1778): French Philosopher and author.

This famous satirist became an enemy early in life of organized authority, especially the royal government and the Church. He wrote a burlesque life of Joan called *La Pucelle* (meaning The Maid, often used as one of Joan's names). His enmity toward Joan of Arc was not personal. Rather, he attacked her as a revered representative of the Church.

FRIEDRICH VON SCHILLER (1759-1805): This noted German dramatist and poet was extremely romantic and idealistic. *Die Jungfrau von Orleans* (The Maid of Orleans), his play about Joan, gives a highly unrealistic portrait. Shaw says that Schiller's Joan is not only unlike the real Joan, but unlike any other real woman who ever lived.

MARK TWAIN (1835-1910): The American author of *Tom Sawyer* and *Huckleberry Finn* became captivated by the story of Joan. He turned her life story into a romance, *The Personal Recollections of Joan of Arc*. Shaw describes this work vividly though not kindly, when he says that Twain's Joan is an American schoolteacher in armor.

ANATOLE FRANCE (1844-1924): A famous French novelist and satirist, Anatole France wrote a study in which he tried to destroy the notion of Joan as a military and political leader. He stated that all her ideas came from others, and her military success was entirely the work of Dunois, who found her useful for raising his soldier's morals, but who led the real fighting himself.

ANDREW LANG (1844-1912): He was a Scottish man of letters. He translated Homer's epics into English, was an important authority on myths and folklore, and collected fairy tales for children. He wrote a book defending Joan after Anatole France's attack.

PROTESTANT MISUNDERSTANDINGS OF THE MIDDLE AGES: To understand Joan of Arc, you must understand the world in which she lived. This is where Mark Twain and Andrew

Lang failed. They were brought up as Protestants; as a result, they had a warped picture of the Catholic Middle Ages.

COMMENT: According to Shaw, there are two weaknesses in books about Joan written by authors with an unconscious Protestant bias. In the first place, such people tend to think of cruel churchmen persecuting heretics of noble character. They therefore picture Joan as a victim and the churchmen who judged her as villains.

If you possess a good understanding of the Middle Ages, Shaw points out, not only do you understand why Joan's accusers acted as they did, but you can even imagine that you yourself would have done the same. In other words, from the viewpoint of those who knew Joan, she was a dangerous person whose behavior attacked the very roots of the Church and the society of the time. A modern reader cannot appreciate Joan's greatness if he does not also understand her dangerousness.

The second weakness of modern Protestant idolators of Joan, Shaw says, is that they automatically assume that the Middle Ages were a barbarous period and things have gotten a great deal better since then. In fact, Shaw feels, the opposite is probably true.

COMPARATIVE FAIRNESS OF JOAN'S TRIAL: At Joan's trial, fifty learned men and two skilled judges spent many weeks in arguing the merits of the case against her. Joan received a much fairer trial than she would receive today.

COMMENT: Shaw illustrates his point by referring to the trials of two modern people who were condemned for their wartime activities and shot.

Edith Cavell was a nurse who helped various Allied prisoners to escape from Belgium to Holland. She was tried by a German court and shot in 1915.

Roger Casement, a British civil servant of great distinction, became an Irish nationalist. In 1916, he went to

Germany to request help of the Germans for an Irish revolution against England. He was convicted of high treason and hanged in London, in 1916.

Although death by shooting or hanging is more humane than burning at the stake, the brief, biased trials received by Edith Cavell and Roger Casement compare very unfavorably with the conscientious trial of Saint Joan. This is the main point of Shaw's discussion here.

JOAN NOT TRIED AS A POLITICAL OFFENDER: Joan was tried by a Church court, not a national court. Her crimes were crimes against the Church, not against the nation. And from the Church's viewpoint, she was undoubtedly guilty. She would not accept the Church's interpretation of God's will instead of her own.

But Joan did not really understand the accusations. Her voices were facts to her. She could not see any relation between these facts and heresy.

COMMENT: Shaw explains the heart of the tragedy as he sees it in this section. His play has no villains. On the one hand there is Joan, very, very young, with enormous natural brilliance, but completely ignorant of the world. On the other hand there is the Church, faced with a heretic who claims personal authority that would be unusual for a Pope. Each of these forces is convinced of its own righteousness, and indeed each one *is* right. But when they clash the impact is terrifying, and Joan is destroyed. We get the full force of the clash in the trial scene of the play. This is pitiful and terrifying because these two forces cannot be reconciled and must meet head on, not because a cruel bishop is persecuting a saintly girl.

This is why Shaw takes such pains in the trial scene to show us the Church's position. The Inquisitor's speech on the dangers of heresy is the longest and, some feel, the finest in the play.

When Bernard Shaw points out that the Church had much trouble with heretics in the Middle Ages, he gives two examples. One was John Wycliffe, an English reformer of Church practices, who lived in the fourteenth century. The other was Jan Hus (1369-1416), a Bohemian critic of the Church. He was burned at the stake as a heretic. Among modern Bohemians (now Czechoslovakians), Hus is revered as the martyred founder of the national Protestant church.

Joan was not simply a reformer, like Wycliffe, Hus, and Martin Luther; she was ready to become the foundation of the Church itself—like Mrs. Eddy, as Shaw puts it. (He refers to Mary Baker Eddy, the founder of Christian Science.)

1381589

Ironically, while Joan's original trial was fair and honest, the inquiry which found her innocent and inspired, twenty-five years later, was corrupt. Charles, who had received his crown from Joan, found it desirable to have Joan's reputation made perfect and Cauchon was conveniently blamed for everything. Thus the honest trial honestly produced a cruelly wrong verdict; the corrupt hearing produced a true verdict. This irony is the basis for the Epilogue to the play.

THE CHURCH UNCOMPROMISED BY ITS AMENDS: While the Church cannot accept the supremacy of private judgment by an individual, it does accept the idea that the highest wisdom may come through a divine revelation to an individual. It is not always easy to distinguish between the two. Therefore a person may seem to be a heretic in his lifetime and later be canonized as a saint.

But all this explanation does not make Joan's burning any less horrible.

COMMENT: In this section Shaw explains how the Church could honestly condemn Joan in the fifteenth century and then canonize her in the twentieth.

This did not discredit the principles on which Joan was condemned. The Church simply said that in Joan's case there was not willful private judgment, but rather divine inspiration.

As he tries to make this clear, Shaw points out in his characteristically unexpected fashion that the dogma of Papal Infallibility is quite a reasonable and flexible concept. One does not expect a writer of Protestant origin and radical views to take such a position. He states that democracies, parliaments, medical societies, and other modern institutions claim far greater infallibility (inability to be wrong) than the Pope ever has claimed. It should be noted that the dogma holds the Pope infallible only in his pronouncements on matters of faith and morals.

CRUELTY, MODERN AND MEDIEVAL: Joan's death was horrible. But innumerable heretics died in the same way, just as many common criminals died by crucifixion, the same as Christ did. Human beings have invented more dreadful methods of execution, and they have been used in comparatively recent times. And prison is perhaps the worst of all.

The Church shared guilt for Joan's horrible death in only one sense. When it excommunicated her, it sentenced her to perpetual imprisonment. This was such a terrible prospect that she chose death instead.

COMMENT: One of Shaw's most earnestly held ideas was that imprisonment is the cruelest, most degrading, most wasteful method of punishing criminals ever invented. He refers to this belief here. He can understand how Joan would rather have been burned alive than imprisoned for life.

CATHOLIC ANTI-CLERICALISM: Many good Catholics have been critical of the clergy. But Joan went beyond this. She almost stated that her soul was no business of the priests: it was only her own concern.

CATHOLICISM NOT YET CATHOLIC ENOUGH: If we feel that

Joan's burning was a regrettable mistake, as we do, it follows
that the Church should broaden itself to include individualists
like her. Then such things could not happen any more.

COMMENT: The title of this section is significant.
"Catholic" literally means "inclusive," "all-embracing."
Yet the Church whose very name indicates its goal of
enfolding all humanity cannot easily include an unusual
human being like Joan. This is dangerous, Shaw indicates,
for the touch of divine inspiration is not always placed on
priests. Indeed, in the past, genius has more often visited
the outcast.

Therefore, the Church must be able to include those who
are in some ways eccentric or difficult; otherwise the
Church itself will be the loser.

Also, Shaw argues, if the Church has perfect confidence
in its doctrines, it will not be afraid to have them questioned, knowing that the questioner must inevitably return to the bosom of the Church. For all roads must lead
there.

THE LAW OF CHANGE IS THE LAW OF GOD: The Church is
a hierarchy, in which the members are sifted and chosen until
the final choice lights on the Pope, the Vicar of Christ. But
God's hand puts greatness upon men with no reference to
their rank or position. For this reason, the Church must make
every effort to accept all who bring unfamiliar ideas.

COMMENT: Here Shaw expounds his belief that society
must accept change and improve itself. This is part of
his belief in Socialism.

Religion, Shaw feels, must welcome the principle of
change if it is to keep the allegiance of modern man. It
cannot oppose change as such. For we have learned that
almost all the ideas which have improved the condition
of mankind were first looked upon as troublesome, eccentric, or heretical. In other words, if another Saint Joan
should come, she would find a church that has learned

to accept her, instead of burning her first and accepting her later.

CREDULITY, MODERN AND MEDIEVAL: When it had the power to do so, the Church would force conformity by persecution. In our time, doctors have more power to coerce the populace than the priests ever had. And they have less conscience about doing so, because they are usually materialists who do not worry about the hereafter.

> **COMMENT:** Once more, Shaw refers to his hatred of vaccination, this time indirectly. That parents should be compelled to have their children vaccinated seems to him outrageous persecution. (See above, Comment on the section of the Preface called "The Modern Education Joan Escaped.")
>
> To most of us, this is sad evidence that Shaw's exceptional intellect had its weak points. The idea of vaccination (injecting vaccines from sick animals) was physically disgusting to him. He never was able to put his prejudices aside long enough to examine the evidence and observe that vaccination does prevent epidemics.

TOLERATION, MODERN AND MEDIEVAL: The question of tolerating unpopular viewpoints is a difficult one. We must draw the line between what is permissible and what is not. Joan's persecutors felt that the spreading of heresy crossed the line—that is, it was criminal, dangerous, and thus intolerable. In the same way, in our time we cannot tolerate unsanitary conditions, because we know they start epidemics.

> **COMMENT:** This section illustrates how fair-minded Shaw tries to be, and how many-sided a view he is capable of presenting. After criticizing the Church for not being more tolerant of unconventional ideas, he now reasonably agrees that no society can tolerate *every* unconventional idea. Some are just too dangerous or too insane. All we can do is to tolerate as much originality as we possibly can, and respect individuality.

VARIABILITY OF TOLERATION: The amount of toleration

society shows at a given time depends on whether society is under pressure. In time of war or fear, cruel persecutions take place. This as true today as in Joan's time. In fact, Joan was treated with remarkable care, considering that it was wartime.

> **COMMENT:** Again Shaw tries to impress upon his readers the idea that society has not necessarily improved between the fifteenth and the twentieth centuries. He points out that modern man still persecutes savagely those who create panic in his breast. He expresses with great vividness the intensity of wartime persecutions: the French government in 1792, he says, cut off people's heads for reasons which in normal times wouldn't have caused a government to chloroform a dog.

THE CONFLICT BETWEEN GENIUS AND DISCIPLINE: The smooth running of our social order is based largely on unquestioning obedience, for most people do not ask for reasons concerning everything they are asked to do. They only require that orders be given by the proper people. A king may give orders to a bishop, but a parish clergyman may not. By normal standards, this farm girl, Joan of Arc, was in a position to give orders to nobody. Yet she gave orders to everybody, including kings.

JOAN AS THEOCRAT: Joan gave her orders as a messenger of God. Therefore, people either accepted her as an agent of the Lord or rejected her as a witch. She was either loved or hated; there was no middle ground.

UNBROKEN SUCCESS ESSENTIAL IN THEOCRACY: Because she was hated as a witch, because she excited the envy and anger of many influential people by her self-righteousness and tactlessness, Joan needed constant worldly triumphs to uphold her. Those who defended her believed she was from God and the saints. Joan's first serious defeat would be bound to destroy faith in her and begin her ruin.

> **COMMENT:** In the above three sections, Shaw discusses the strengths and weaknesses Joan created when she claimed to speak for God. On the one hand, this gave her

the courage to speak out of turn to the very highest. It
gave her adulation from those who regarded her as a
heavenly messenger. But it also earned her the hatred of
those whose worldly importance she ignored. It made her
very vulnerable. For as soon as she was defeated, her position as one sent by Heaven was destroyed.

MODERN DISTORTIONS OF JOAN'S HISTORY: This Preface
is necessary because a fair, sober statement about Joan's career
does not exist. Though most reference books are correct about
the events and dates concerned with her life, they all make
Cauchon a villain.

COMMENT: Shaw intends the Preface to *Saint Joan* as a
corrective to the unfair accounts of Joan's trial current
at the time he was writing (1924). We must bear in
mind that Joan had been made a saint in 1920, and the
world was still echoing from that event. Glorification of
Joan was in the air. And to most people, glorification of
Joan meant the blackening of Cauchon's reputation. Only
Shaw saw a sadder, more complicated struggle behind
Joan's death and sainthood. To Shaw, there are romance,
tragedy, and comedy in her story. For it is the story of
the great human being—the Superman—and the ordinary people of the world who do their limited best. The
way the ordinary man treats the Superman is wasteful,
destructive, sad, and funny.

HISTORY ALWAYS OUT OF DATE: Usually, lies are told about
important people in their own time, but after centuries pass,
the truth is told. However, in Joan's case, lies are still being
told.

COMMENT: In this section the author enumerates the
various reasons why history has not yet told the truth
about Joan. People who are anticlerical (that is, who
disapprove of priests, ministers, and all other representa-
tives of organized religion) find it useful to picture Joan
as the victim of that vicious churchman, Cauchon. Protestants use Joan's story to illustrate the intolerance and
cruelty of the Catholic Church. Roman Catholics do not

care to discuss the fact that Joan was very nearly a Protestant. He himself, he indicates, is offering the unvarnished truth about Joan.

Of course, we must bear in mind as we follow Shaw's argument that he is presenting only one version of the truth. His explanation of Joan's life and death is most carefully thought out and is the result of painstaking study. But it is not the only possible explanation.

THE REAL JOAN NOT MARVELOUS ENOUGH FOR US: We find it hard to accept the real Joan. This is not because we are less willing to believe in strange and marvelous stories than the people of the fifteenth century were. We have a much greater capacity for believing fantastic things. Look how we believe in the stories astronomers tell us about the hugeness of the stars, or what physicists tell us about the smallness of the atom. Joan is not too marvelous for us; the trouble is, she is not marvelous enough.

COMMENT: It must be noted that Shaw is not stating that what scientists tell us is untrue. He does not question the accuracy of what we are told. He merely says that it takes a flexible imagination to grasp it and believe it.

At the same time, the tone of the passage suggests a sneering attitude. Shaw's offhand reference to electrons, "whatever they may be," shows that if there is something he knows nothing about, he cannot help assuming that it is not worth knowing. Shaw does not show any appreciation of the rigorous nature of scientific thought.

THE STAGE LIMITS OF HISTORICAL REPRESENTATION: The play *Saint Joan* contains the happenings of more than a year, compressed into three and one-half hours. Therefore, the play makes things happen a lot faster than they did in real life. Also, the characters in the play are invented, to conform to the deeds of the real people who figured in Joan's histories—a necessity, since we do not know much about their characters.

COMMENT: With this section, Shaw begins the last part

of his Preface. He turns from a consideration of Joan's life to a discussion of his play. The remainder of the Preface will concern the play itself.

Here, Shaw, points out that he is, after all, writing a play, not a history. For the purposes of the stage, he must edit and rearrange historical events to some degree. For instance, he shows Joan being tried, excommunicated, temporarily saved, and finally executed, all in about a half hour.

It is difficult, Shaw points out, to know what the people involved in Joan's story were really like. He has guessed at this. These guesses do not pretend to be historically accurate portraits. Shakespeare made the same kind of guess in his plays, whenever he portrayed a character who had existed in real life.

To summarize, Shaw is saying that his readers should not feel triumphant if they discover he is not accurate in some details of the play. He knows this perfectly well.

A VOID IN THE ELIZABETHAN DRAMA: Shaw feels he has one important advantage over Shakespeare. He has what may be called historical sense. Shakespeare had none. That is, Shaw knows about the backgrounds of the characters in the play—the sort of social institutions that existed in their time, and he makes this a factor in the play. Shakespeare's characters are individuals who exist without any reference to their times.

COMMENT: Shakespeare (note that Shaw always uses the spelling "Shakespear") is a favorite subject for Shaw's commentary. While Shaw knew and appreciated Shakespeare's plays almost all his life, he was always troubled by Shakespeare's emphasis on individual personalities. Shakespeare did not show social pressures at work on human beings. He was interested mainly in their characters as people. Shaw felt this was a sign that Shakespeare did not care about the analysis and reform of human society.

Here he brings up this point once more. (He previously discussed it at length in "Better Than Shakespear?", an early preface written in connection with his play *Caesar and Cleopatra*.) He understands the nature of medieval society, Shaw claims, whereas the characters in those plays of Shakespeare which are set in the Middle Ages show no medieval characteristics at all. For instance, John of Gaunt might be a man of Shakespeare's own time.

NOTE: John of Gaunt is a character in Shakespeare's play *Richard II*, written in the 1590's. The action of that play occurs at the end of the fourteenth century. John of Gaunt makes a famous speech in which he praises the beauty and glory of England. This emotional love of England was common in Shakespeare's time, but it did not exist in the Middle Ages. Shaw comments that Gaunt's speech might better have come from Sir Francis Drake, a famous English admiral of Shakespeare's own time.

In other words, Shaw points out that the characters in *Saint Joan* speak with the voices of the Middle Ages. None of Shakespeare's characters ever do this.

TRAGEDY, NOT MELODRAMA: The play has no villain. The evil deeds of villains are less interesting than the wrongs that decent people do in good faith.

COMMENT: The idea developed at length in earlier sections of the Preface (see Comment on the section titled "Joan Not Tried As A Political Offender," above) is here briefly referred to once more. The play gives a fair portrayal of the men who destroyed Joan. They acted from righteous motives. They murdered, but they were not murderers.

THE INEVITABLE FLATTERIES OF TRAGEDY: In the case of Cauchon and Le Maitre the Inquisitor, it has been necessary to make them better men than they probably really were. They have been unfairly abused so often that one must now flatter them somewhat to restore the balance.

Also, both of these, as well as the Duke of Warwick, must be shown as understanding and explaining their own actions far more clearly than they would in real life.

COMMENT: This is one of the key sections of the Preface. Shaw explains the reasons for some of the unusual features, which are always a shock when one first sees or reads *Saint Joan*—the manner in which the bishop who prosecutes Joan is shown as a courageous, scrupulously conscientious churchman, and the inquisitor is a kindly, soft-spoken, scholarly man.

Shaw realizes that he is overemphasizing the virtues of these men. But if he is to tell the truth about the kind of trial Joan received, he must do this.

Even more subtle and interesting is Shaw's idea of having the characters (Cauchon, the Inquisitor, Warwick) explain themselves. Only in this way can he explain them to the audience. In real life, a man does not see himself with the striking clarity of these characters in the play. But as Shaw unforgettably expresses it, by sacrificing "verisimilitude" he gains "veracity." That is, by purposely failing to copy the blind ignorance most men show about their own behavior, Shaw manages to exhibit the inner truth about Joan's life and death. His play is not realistic, but it tells the truth.

SOME WELL-MEANT PROPOSALS FOR IMROVING THE PLAY: Some critics, even those who admire the play, have helpfully suggested that the play could be made a lot shorter by taking out the Epilogue, as well as all material dealing with the Church, heresy, and feudalism.

This is not so. The producers would immediately put in enormous battle scenes, coronation scenes, and execution scenes, which would take a long time to set up on the stage and a long time to perform. Thus the play would end up being just as long, but it would be slow and dreary.

COMMENT: This witty, good-natured jest at the critics

(some of whom did not like what Shaw considered to be
the heart of the play) effortlessly disposes of their rather
absurd attempts to tell him how to do his job. Of course,
Saint Joan without the discussions of the reasons for
Joan's fate, would be a thin, ordinary play. But Shaw
does not denounce his critics with explosive anger; rather,
he uses amiable ridicule to make them look foolish.

At the same time, Shaw's joke has a grain of truth in it.
Many productions of Shakespeare, especially those in
Shaw's time, cut out large portions of the plays in order
to include much unnecessary spectacle. Shaw knew this
could someday happen to his play too. For this reason,
he urges the reader to see the play while he (Shaw) is
still alive.

THE EPILOGUE: The Epilogue is important. For the burning
of Joan does not matter as much as what happened afterward.

COMMENT: Some critics did not care for the epilogue,
saying that it spoiled the tragic tone of the great trial
scene. Shaw flatly insists on its importance.

There is no doubt that the Epilogue carries the message
of the drama and sums up many of the ideas which are
scattered through the play. Also, it is a very fine scene
in its own right, combining comedy, intellectual force,
and beauty. It can be criticized as lightening the deeply
tragic coloring of the previous scene.

TO THE CRITICS, LEST THEY SHOULD FEEL IGNORED: Many
people who go to the theatre hate it. Critics hate it because
they are paid to put up with it. Many fashionable people at-
tend in order to show off their clothes, have something to
talk about, or for other irrelevant reasons. For such people,
a play cannot be short enough.

But Shaw writes for people who love the theatre, not for those
who hate it. Therefore, he presents without apology this
three-and-one-half-hour drama.

COMMENT: This final section of the Preface is Shaw's final defense of his play. He is convinced that those criticisms which suggest that large parts of the play be removed are only complaints about giving concentrated attention to what he has to say for three and a half hours. At the root of the matter is the fact that many critics (and other playgoers) hate the drama.

Note Shaw's amusing paraphrase of most modern drama criticism. It is instructive to take a few play reviews at random from the daily papers and compare them with this. All too often, the critic really is saying he hates long plays, he hates to think, and he wants to get home as fast as possible, just as Shaw claims.

Shaw also points out that many people in the world do not feel this way. They stand in line for tickets. In some parts of the world, they sit through plays lasting for twelve hours, or even a week. These are not necessarily fashionable or even educated people, but they are the ones that matter to a writer of plays.

NOTE: In connection with this, Ober-Ammergau is mentioned. This is a town in Austria where a Passion Play, a play depicting the death of Christ, has been presented for generations. The production is staged and acted entirely by the townspeople themselves. The play takes an entire day to perform.

Shaw concludes with a few genial remarks to the unhappy playgoers who don't want to see any more play than they can help. He suggests that they can come late to *Saint Joan* and leave early. They can even stay at home. But he hopes they will not do that. His finances will suffer. Besides, they may be pleasantly surprised: they may find that what matters is not how long a play lasts, but how quickly the time seems to pass.

GENERAL REMARKS ON THE PREFACE: Sometimes, Bernard Shaw's prefaces have little relevance to the plays they are attached to. Shaw simply uses the play as a jumping off place for a discussion of things only distantly related to it. The Preface to *Saint Joan* is not of this type. It intimately concerns the play itself. It is an essay which examines and interprets the historical events of Joan's life and death. Therefore it may be described as the raw material of research and thought out of which the play was made. Shaw himself puts it very well when he says that the prose of Joan's life is in the Preface, while the poetry of it is in the play.

While the Preface is not free of repetitions, it has a clear, well-proportioned structure. It begins with a thorough examination of Joan herself—her life, the social class from which she came, her genius, her weaknesses, even her appearance. Then, having pictured Joan, the essay proceeds to examine fifteenth-century France with its mighty components, the Church and the feudal system. It gives special emphasis to the role of the Church in Joan's life and death.

At last, Shaw turns away from the subject matter of the play and gives his attention to the play itself, defending *Saint Joan* vigorously but unemotionally from its critics and from the well-meaning persons who have been telling him how to improve it.

Throughout, the essay is peppered with deflating remarks indicating that the twentieth century is no better than the fifteenth, and in fact is in certain ways worse.

The play stands magnificently by itself. Yet one's understanding and enjoyment are increased by a careful reading of the Preface.

THE MAIN CHARACTERS IN THE PLAY

Joan of Arc

Robert de Baudricourt—commander of the castle of Vaucouleurs who first sends Joan to the Dauphin.

The Dauphin of France—later crowned as Charles VII through Joan's efforts.

The Archbishop of Rheims—a worldly churchman present at the Dauphin's court.

La Trémouille—an arrogant nobleman who is in command of the French army until Joan's arrival.

Gilles de Rais—a courtier.

Captain La Hire—a rough-talking soldier who becomes devoted to Joan.

Dunois, Bastard of Orléans—commander of the garrison at Orléans, who becomes Joan's comrade in arms and friend.

Richard de Beauchamp, Earl of Warwick—English nobleman concerned in the capture and execution of Joan.

Chaplain de Stogumber—English priest, a follower of Warwick, who hates Joan passionately.

Peter Cauchon, Bishop of Beauvais—churchman who takes a leading part in Joan's trial and conviction.

The Inquisitor—a high Church official concerned with the prosecution of heresy, associated with Cauchon at Joan's trial.

Canon de Courcelles—an unintelligent churchman who is Stogumber's ally at the trial.

Canon d'Estivet—Joan's prosecutor at the trial.

Brother Martin Ladvenu—a priest present at the trial who becomes converted to her cause at the time of her death.

The Executioner of Rouen

THE SCENES: The play is not divided into acts. It is a chronicle (a history play) in six scenes showing six important stages of Joan's career and an epilogue which takes place after her death. It was Shaw's intention that the play be performed with only one intermission.

SCENE I

It is the year 1429; the scene is a chamber in the castle of Vaucouleurs. Its commander, Robert de Baudricourt, is abusing his steward because there are no eggs. The steward explains that the farm animals are bewitched because of a girl who is waiting outside. When Baudricourt interviews her, she amazes him by telling him that she has come at God's orders to raise the siege of Orléans. She will need a horse, armor, and an escort to take her to the Dauphin. More surprising still, several of the noblemen at the castle have already agreed to accompany her.

COMMENT: The play opens in a low key. From the pleasant little comedy between Baudricourt and his steward, one receives little suggestion of the exalted material to come. Baudricourt blusters while the steward squirms (a steward being the supervisor of a household or estate), and only when the steward explains that the Maid from Domrémy has bewitched the hens and the cows, do we touch upon the real material of the scene.

Shaw gives some description of Joan before she actually appears. Baudricourt recalls he has already ordered the steward to throw the girl out of the castle and send her home to her father for a beating. The steward has not done this, though he is very much afraid of Baudricourt. His only explanation for his disobedience is that the girl will not go, and "she is so positive." In other words, we see that Joan has prevailed by the power of her character, without the aid of any physical force.

The audience gets an opportunity to see Joan when Baudricourt orders her into his presence. She is a strong country girl of perhaps seventeen, in a red dress. This is the only time in the play that we see her in woman's clothes. Though pious and knowledgeable about house and farm, she lacks any kind of polish or book learning.

Shaw represents this by having her speak an English country dialect. For instance, she asks Baudricourt: "Be you captain?"

Nevertheless, she is clearly a remarkable person. Her face shows power and imagination. Her handling of Baudricourt is astonishing. She is not at all disrespectful. Yet, within a few minutes she is giving orders to him. His loudest anger has no effect on her. She radiates a calm, cheerful confidence. She rides over his objections like a steamroller. She does not ask him to arrange her trip to the Dauphin at Chinon. She has already done that herself. He has only to agree.

Joan astonishes Baudricourt most of all by announcing that Squire Bertrand de Poulengey is willing to go with her. Poulengey is obviously a man whose opinions carry some weight. Joan is ordered to wait outside while Baudricourt speaks to Poulengey, who is informally known as Polly to his friends.

Baudricourt assumes that Polly must have an ulterior motive for his interest in Joan. Polly assures him this is not so. Polly has been moved by the girl. He hopes the same may happen to the Dauphin and the French army. At any rate, it is worth trying, for this is the only chance they have.

COMMENT: Poulengey—"Polly"—is an entirely different type of a person from Baudricourt. He is slow, quiet, thoughtful, and stubborn; in contrast, Baudricourt is noisy, quick-tempered, and not really very sure of himself. Poulengey is the more imposing of the two. Indirectly, we find Joan more impressive because she has been able to impress a man like Poulengey. We also note that Joan is able to affect two completely different men. Thus we begin to see that her power has great range.

At first, the only logical reason Baudricourt can think of for Polly's amazing attitude toward Joan is that he wants to carry her off and seduce her, under the pretense of taking her to the Dauphin. By Poulengey's solemn denial,

we learn that Joan's effect is on men's minds, their imaginations, their untouched possibilities, not upon their
sexual impulses. This is reinforced when Poulengey states
that not one improper remark has been made to Joan by
the usually foul-mouthed common soldiers.

In this same conversation, Baudricourt adds to our information about Joan. He tells Polly that her father is an
important farmer in the district, a man who might have
relatives in the church or the legal profession, and who
therefore could make trouble if anything happened to his
daughter. That is, Joan does not come from the humblest,
poorest social class, but from prosperous people of some
local importance. Shaw tries to make this very clear
because romantic stories about Joan often describe her
inaccurately as a poor shepherd girl.

One reason Poulengey supports Joan is that the French
position is so desperate. The situation could not be much
worse, he figures; anything is worth trying. In connection
with this, he describes the current situation. The English,
together with the Duke of Burgundy (who has rebelled
against the French crown and supports the English),
hold half of France, including Paris. The Dauphin will
not fight. His own mother has said that he is illegitimate
and has no right to the throne.

At this time (1429), the English were still enjoying the
results of the victories won by their warrior king, Henry
V, who died in 1422. By the Treaty of Troyes (1420), the
French king disinherited his own son, the Dauphin, made
Henry V the heir to the French throne, and gave Henry
his daughter Catherine in marriage. Henry died unex-
pectedly two years later. The French king died at almost
the same time. The Dauphin ignored the humiliating
Treaty of Troyes and claimed the crown. But seven years
later, he was still not formally crowned. He remained
Dauphin instead of king. ("Dauphin" was the title always
given to the heir to the French throne.)

Baudricourt questions Joan once more, about the saints' voices

she claims to hear, as well as about her plans. He is flabber-
gasted to learn that she intends to follow her intended victory
at Orléans by crowning the Dauphin at Rheims cathedral and
driving the English from French soil. She explains her idea
about men belonging in their own country. She also describes
what is wrong with the French army and how it can be made
to fight. Baudricourt agrees to let her go to Chinon.

COMMENT: Joan will not tell Baudricourt anything
about how her saints' voices come to her. This foreshadows
her later refusal to discuss the matter at all. Historically,
Joan did steadfastly refrain from answering questions
about her voices. She said she did not have their per-
mission. Baudricourt states that the voices come from
Joan's imagination. Joan agrees—for that, she says, is how
God's messages come to us. (Shaw discusses Joan's voices
at length in the Preface. He comes to the conclusion that
she was a vividly imaginative person who received her
ideas in the form of words said to her by voices. Thus, to
Shaw, it is true that Joan received God's message through
her imagination. Her own genius spoke to her this way,
and Shaw feels that human genius is truly a divine voice.)

Joan feels that the war against the English is a holy war.
The English belong in their own country, England. France
is the place meant for the French. When one country tries
to conquer another, the invaders are possessed of the
devil and do many wicked things. This makes no sense
to Baudricourt: A man's loyalty is to his feudal lord, and
it makes no difference who the lord is or what language
he speaks.

Baudricourt speaks for the feudal social order, which is
approaching its end. The feudal system is international,
for loyalty is built upon social classes, not upon nationality.
Joan represents nationalism, in which loyalty to a country and a language supersedes the feudal loyalties. She
speaks for a new European social order which was just
being born in her time.

Joan's theory of war is closely connected with her ideas

about nationalism. Why' do French soldiers lose battles? Why are they demoralized? Joan answers, because they have nothing to fight for. The common soldier tries not to get killed. The knight is only interested in taking a wealthy prisoner and securing a large ransom. Joan will teach them to put aside these selfish motives and fight so that God's will may be done in France. If each man willingly puts his life in God's hands at the start of a battle they will defeat the English easily.

Joan here anticipates a later realism in the conduct of war. Shaw states that Napoleon developed a war method similar to Joan's—namely, that if a battle is worth giving lives for, the only way to win is to pay the price.

To summarize, in this short first scene, Joan clearly displays those habits of thought which show her to be the apostle of Protestantism (her voices are between herself and God, and they are nobody else's business) and of nationalism (loyalty to one's land and language is more important than loyalty to one's feudal superior). These tendencies are at the center of her greatness. They also are the cause of her destruction.

After Joan leaves with Poulengey, the steward returns with a basket of eggs. The hens are laying again. Baudricourt is overcome by reverence. He is now sure that Joan came from God.

COMMENT: We must not make the mistake of taking this "miracle" seriously. That such trivialities as the laying of hens' eggs should cause the rise of faith is an absurdity to Shaw. This is a measure of Baudricourt's brainlessness and insensitivity. He is hesitant in his response to the strength and brilliance of Joan. But he becomes a reverent worshiper when his steward brings him some eggs. An unimportant coincidence does what the power of Joan's genius cannot.

SCENE II

The scene is in an antechamber at the castle in Chinon. The

Archbishop of Rheims and La Trémouille are awaiting the Dauphin. Gilles de Rais joins them, followed shortly by Captain La Hire. La Hire, whose habit of swearing is well known, has just undergone a sudden reformation. A soldier known as Foul Mouthed Frank has just fallen into a well and drowned, just after an "angel" dressed as a soldier told him not to use such language when he was at the point of death. With a tremendous oath, La Hire swears never to swear again, to the amusement of the others!

COMMENT: The scene begins with a conversation about the Dauphin. La Trémouille and the Archbishop both exhibit contempt for him. We learn that he is shabby and in debt to both of them.

Gilles de Rais, known as Bluebeard, like everyone else in the play, was a real person. In 1440, eleven years after this scene, he was tried and hanged for murdering large numbers of children for sadistic pleasure. Shaw refers briefly to his later history in the description he gives when de Rais first appears in this scene.

From de Rais and La Hire we learn that Joan has arrived. She is of course the angel in soldier's dress. Again a coincidence has made converts to her cause. After all, Foul Mouthed Frank was warned innumerable times about his swearing. Finally he has fallen into a well—not remarkable, since he was a drunkard. When Joan told him he was on the point of death, she meant that all men are, since any man may die at any moment. But the combination of circumstances profoundly impresses the rough soldier La Hire. He becomes Joan's devoted follower from this point on.

Charles, the Dauphin, enters. La Trémouille, the Archbishop, and Bluebeard all treat him with offhand rudeness. The Archbishop even refers openly to the stories that Charles is not the legitimate son of the late king.

Charles flourishes a letter from Baudricourt, about an angel whom Baudricourt is sending to Chinon. The Archbishop and

La Trémouille are hostile at first, but agains the hopelessness of the situation works in Joan's favor; they decide to admit her to the Dauphin's presence.

To test whether she will recognize the blood royal, the Dauphin decides to hide among the courtiers while Gilles de Rais poses as the Dauphin. The Archbishop explains to La Trémouille that Joan will identify the Dauphin without difficulty: both his description and that of Bluebeard are well known.

> **COMMENT:** The Archbishop, who is a worldly man, and more intelligent than La Trémouille, understands beforehand that Joan will have no trouble identifying the Dauphin, for everyone knows that the Dauphin is the poorest looking man at the court, and that Gilles de Rais has a little beard dyed blue. La Trémouille says that then, of course, there will be no miracle.
>
> On the contrary, the bishop replies, it will be a miracle. It will create faith, and whatever helps to create faith is a miracle. La Trémouille is certain that there is something wrong with this argument, but he is not subtle enough to figure out what it is. The conversation serves to make clear the distinction between the two men, the soldier of fierce disposition and dull mind, and the churchman, more shrewd than holy.

The curtains of the anteroom are drawn apart to reveal the full court. Joan easily recognizes Bluebeard and picks out Charles. She is overcome with religious fervor before the Archbishop. He is shamed by her adoration, but moved by her deep piety. He asserts that she comes from God.

> **COMMENT:** In the play, the Archbishop becomes convinced of Joan's genuineness within a few minutes. In real life, Joan was examined by various clergymen for weeks before she was accepted.
>
> Joan's excited reverence toward the Archbishop has a double purpose. It shames his worldly wisdom; a few

minutes previously he was explaining Joan with assurance, but now she turns out to be something different from what he so confidently expected. Also, the Archbishop is alarmed at the passion of Joan's religious feeling. He tells her she is in love with religion. This is not wrong, but it is dangerous. This is a brief foreshadowing of Joan's short future and violent end.

At Joan's request, she is left alone with the Dauphin. He is frightened and unwilling, but she overrides all his objections, and at last he calls the court together and, before them all, gives the command of the army to Joan. He even finds the courage to defy La Trémouille, or old Gruff-and-Grum, as Joan calls him. The knights of the court become inflamed by Joan's enthusiasm and pledge to follow her to Orléans.

COMMENT: The scene between the Dauphin and Joan is entirely Shaw's invention. In real life, Joan would never reveal what she said to the Dauphin to win him over, so that Shaw had to construct the dialogue by which a weak and selfish man was persuaded to rise above his fear and laziness. That Joan did persuade Charles in real life to take the incredible step of putting the army in her command is an amazing fact. It remained for Shaw to imagine in a convincing way how the dedicated peasant girl inspired the Dauphin to cast off his inertia and follow her lead.

Joan's speech to the Dauphin is always affectionate and startlingly informal. She calls him Charlie and addresses him as "thou." (This is the familiar form of address. "You" is the form of formal address. We no longer pay attention to this distinction in English, though it is still used in French and German.)

Charles is pictured as a man who is out of place in the violent world of medieval politics. He is not physically suited to fighting. He complains that the armor is too heavy for him and he can hardly lift the sword. Also, the idea of killing is uncongenial to him. He is a kindly man, if kindliness does not interfere with his personal comfort. For Charles likes comfort. He wants safety and a comfortable bed far more than he wants honor and glory. In a way, Charles is ahead of his time. He understands that fighting is not the sensible way to settle disputes. Using one's brain is better.

Joan handles Charles with a masterly blend of coaxing and gentle bullying. There are in her the makings of a managing woman. Shaw remarks in the Preface that if she had lived a long life she would have turned into the same type of woman as Queen Elizabeth I of England. To each of Charles's objections, she has an answer. He wants to be let alone, and anyway, he is sure a treaty will be better than a battle. He feels that the English are stupid and can easily be outsmarted at the conference table. But Joan answers that if the English are victorious, they will make the treaty, and "then God help poor France." There is nothing to do except to stand up and fight. It does not matter whether Charles wants to, or whether he cares about being King at all; God has put the burden on him, and he must see it through.

Especially effective is Joan's scornful reply when Charles wants them both to mind their own business. Her words are rough but her tone is exalted. The idea of minding one's business she calls "muck." It is God's business that Charles and Joan must do. In Rheims cathedral, Charles is to be crowned. There he must give France to God; then he will become God's steward and God's servant. That is what it means to be King of France.

Charles is carried away by this noble vision of the monarchy. He reassembles the court so all may hear him give command of the army to the Maid. He even manages (with Joan's encouraging hand on his shoulder) to snap his fingers in the face of the furious La Trémouille. All the knights are moved by Joan's cry: "Who is for God and His Maid?" They will follow her to Orléans.

However, there are troubling undertones to Joan's

triumph at Chinon. Charles agrees to risk supporting
Joan. But he knows his own character. He realizes that
he is not a fighter, and that he hates inconvenience more
than anything. He warns Joan at the very moment of
his decision that he will not be able to keep it up. Already we realize that when Joan needs support, Charles
will not be resolute enough to give it to her.

SCENE III

It is April 29, 1429. The scene is the south shore of the river
Loire, at Orléans. Dunois and his page are watching the
water in the evening breeze.

> COMMENT: Jean, Comte de Dunois, was the illegitimate
> son of the Duke of Orléans. This was the reason for
> his nickname, the Bastard of Orléans. Though such a
> reference may seem tactless, to say the least, the Middle
> Ages did not feel that way. In those days, it was very
> common to give people names which referred openly
> to their handicaps.

> Shaw mentions that Dunois' shield shows a bend sinister.
> A bend is a pair of diagonal parallel lines across the
> shield. Normally, the bend goes from the upper right
> to the lower left. When it goes the opposite way (from
> upper left to lower right), it is called the bend sinister
> (sinister here has its original meaning of "left") and
> denotes illegitimacy.

As Dunois waits for the Maid, whom he has not yet seen,
he watches the beautiful blue kingfishers flying over the
bushes on the opposite shore.

> COMMENT: This is a rare moment of stillness and poetic
> beauty in the play. It provides a pause and a contrast
> amid the scenes of intrigue and battle.

Joan arrives, full of eagerness to start an immediate attack.
Dunois explains the military situation. An attack will do
no good. The English hold two impregnable forts guarding

the bridge to Orléans. To take the forts, the French must cross the Loire and attack them from the rear. But a west wind is needed, and for days an east wind has been blowing. Dunois shows Joan his lance, stuck in the ground, with a flag on it which streams westward, showing an east wind is blowing.

Joan starts for the church to pray for a change in the wind. Dunois accompanies her. The page picks up the shield to follow them, but as he is about to take the lance, he notices that the wind is now blowing from the west. Wildly excited, he calls Dunois and Joan. Dunois crosses himself, kneels, and hands his commander's baton to Joan; she is now his leader. They head for the forts to begin the attack.

COMMENT: This scene makes clear the relationship between Dunois and Joan. She is inexperienced. Dunois gives her the guidance and the restraint she needs, for if it were not for Dunois, Joan would throw herself into battle without any planning or caution. From Joan, Dunois gets the conviction that God is on their side, since He has sent the Maid and changed the wind. Joan is so moved when the moment comes that she has worked for that she bursts into tears, and Dunois must lead her by the arm to the wall of the fort.

SCENE IV

COMMENT: The scene is the English camp. This is the only scene in the play in which Joan does not appear. Yet the scene is about her, though she is not in it.

There is no action here. The Earl of Warwick and the Bishop of Beauvais meet to discuss the intended execution of Joan. Their discussion carries much of the intellectual weight of the play. Three persons take part in the scene. Their characters are differentiated with care and much skill.

The English commander, Richard de Beauchamp, Earl of Warwick, is an experienced military commander, diplomat, and courtier. His manners are polished. His intelligence is cool, shrewd, and entirely cynical. He will do whatever is necessary to help his side. He has come to the decision that it is desirable for Joan to be burnt as a witch, and here he efficiently begins to organize for that result.

Peter Cauchon, Bishop of Beauvais, is about sixty years old. His political sympathies have been with the English. As a result, followers of Joan have expelled him from his diocese. All this makes Warwick assume that Cauchon will gladly conspire with him to destroy Joan.

But Cauchon has a side that Warwick has not figured on. He is a serious churchman who feels his responsibilities. To Cauchon, there are two matters which must receive conscientious consideration. First comes the wiping out of Joan's heresy, for heresy can endanger many human souls and even the church itself. Second, every effort must be made to save Joan's soul, now periled by eternal damnation.

Also present at the discussion is Chaplain John de Stogumber, an English priest. He is so outraged by English defeats at Joan's hands that he is consumed with hatred of her. She is an enemy of England. Therefore she must be a witch. Therefore she must burn. To de Stogumber, it is as simple as that. He is not concerned with fine points of theology; he does not care whether Joan is a witch or a heretic, so long as she dies for it. As Cauchon says, the English priest is "strangely blunt in the mind."

The discussion here is lengthy and intensive. This is one of the sections which some critics have suggested cutting out of the play. For Shaw's amusing but firm refusal to consider any such thing, see the final three sections of the Preface.

Without doubt, this scene makes exceptional demands upon the actors who play the roles of Warwick and Cauchon. They must be continuously clear and interest-

ing. They have to preserve the organization and shape
of Shaw's thought. Also, they must project this to the
audience. In other words, they need to highly intelligent
and well trained—qualities perhaps best found in the
trained Shakespearean actor.

Shaw does give the actors a great deal of help: the
language is flexible and precise; there is contrast between
the two men, so that interplay of personalities goes on
at the same time as the combat of ideas. But the greatest
help of all is the presence of de Stogumber. Because he
is so impenetrably stupid, the two others find it necessary to halt their abstract discussion at intervals and
explain in terms that he can understand. His interrup-
tions provoke lively reactions in Warwick and Cauchon,
ranging from amusement to fury to weary acceptance
of his mental limitations. This serves to vary the tone
and mood of the scene. In other words, there is a human
comedy which exists together with the intellectual drama.

Besides this, Shaw uses de Stogumber to satirize the
mental outlook and conventional ideas of the average
Englishman. He thus provides a necessary comic contrast to the essentially serious material of the scene.

As the scene opens, Warwick is calmly admiring a book—not
reading it, just admiring it. De Stogumber is upset, for things
have been going badly with the English since their defeat
at Orléans; they have just suffered a particularly bad reverse
at Patay. De Stogumber feels this as an Englishman; he
cannot accept defeat from a French witch and her followers.
Warwick expresses irritation at this emphasis on "English"
and "French." He recognizes a threat to feudalism and the
Church if loyalty to one's native land should come into
fashion.

COMMENT: In real life, very few people display the fore-
sight and talent for political analysis that Warwick
displays here. The real Warwick no doubt failed to
realize the implications of Joan's emphasis on nationalism. But Shaw explains that it is necessary in a play to

have people understand themselves and their society
far better than people really do, so that they may make
all clear to the audience. See the section of the Preface
entitled, "The Inevitable Flatteries of Tragedy."

Cauchon enters. Warwick, after a carefully courteous greet-
ing, explains that Charles will shortly be crowned at Rheims,
and that the English are unable to prevent it. Stogumber's
view is that Joan must be a witch, since she has beaten the
English, and beating the English is impossible by normal
means.

COMMENT: We have here a good example of the way
Stogumber's presence turns an abstract discussion into
concrete channels. Stogumber cites the fact that Joan
has captured Sir John Talbot, the English commander
at Patay. This proves she is a sorceress. Cauchon points
out that Talbot is a fierce soldier but a thoroughly in-
competent general. Warwick agrees with him.

Cauchon rejects the notion that Joan is a witch; he points out
that she has not claimed to perform any miracles. She is a
heretic. She claims direct communication with God, without
the intervention of the Church. This is a threat to all of
Christendom.

COMMENT: Cauchon, again with an insight which would
not be likely in real life, recognizes Joan as one of the
breed of Mohammed, Wycliffe (pronounced by Cauchon
as "Wc Leef"), and Hus. (For information on Wycliffe
and Hus, see Comment on the section of the Preface
titled, "Comparative Fairness of Joan's Trial.")

Mohammed, born in the city of Mecca about 580 A.D.,
was the founder of the Mohammedan religion. According
to the tenets of that faith, Mohammed heard the voice
of the angel Gabriel, who inspired him to speak as the
prophet of God.

Warwick is not impressed by the danger of Joan's religious
heresy. But he is concerned over her secular heresy. Joan

wished all kings to give their kingdoms to God and reign as His deputies. But to Warwick, the lands really belong to the peers, not the king. Once the land is looked on as the king's, where will the barons be? They will lose their power. In turn, Cauchon does not appear too concerned by this possibility.

> **COMMENT:** The high churchmen and the great feudal barons were traditional rivals in the struggle for power. Warwick knows that if the barons are weakened, the Church hierarchy will be the stronger for it. Cauchon knows that Warwick would not be sorry to see churchmen lose some of the tremendous influence they wield; the barons could go their way unchecked. Thus the two are natural enemies. They come together temporarily to crush Joan, who threatens both of them.

Warwick names Joan's religious heresy, in which the individual communes with heaven without the intercession of the Church, "Protestantism." Cauchon names Joan's political heresy, in which the individual subject serves the king without reference to the nobles, "Nationalism." They agree upon the necessity of burning her. Cauchon emphasizes again that first every effort will be made to save Joan's soul. Warwick agrees that the horror of burning at the stake should be avoided if possible. Only Stogumber is without pity.

> **COMMENT:** Again Shaw departs from realism in the interest of historical clarity. It is completely unlikely that the terms "Protestantism" and "Nationalism" could have been neatly invented on this occasion. But this does serve to make clear the medieval forces that Joan antagonized and the reasons why they felt she was dangerous.

Note the final contrast between de Stogumber and the two others. Cauchon is a scrupulous man who will do his duty to Joan and save her if he can. Even Warwick does not enjoy the prospect of burning a human being alive. But de Stogumber says he would burn the girl with his own hands. Cauchon shows great insight when he blesses him with the comment "Sancta simplicitas" (holy sim-

plicity, in the sense of stupidity). Cauchon realizes that
de Stogumber is not cruel, only brainless and unimagi-
native.

Finally, we must bear in mind that this scene tells us
indirectly of Joan's progress. She has seized the imagination of the French people. Warwick speaks of a cult of
the Maid. She is now important enough to be of concern
to powerful men like Warwick and Cauchon.

SCENE V

The scene is set in the ambulatory (gallery or corridor) of
the Cathedral at Rheims. Charles has just been crowned King
of France. Jean, dressed in magnificent armor, is kneeling alone
at prayer. She is joined by Dunois. Dunois explains to her that
she has many enemies—which surprises and bewilders her,
since her intentions are completely unselfish. In a confiding
moment, Joan explains to him about her voices; she hears
them in the church bells.

COMMENT: The theme of Scene V is the loneliness of
Joan. It's tone is sad and chill. There is fine irony in the
fact that Joan's aloneness becomes apparent just at the
time when she triumphantly reaches her objective of
having Charles crowned at Rheims.

Dunois has true affection for Joan. He warns her that she
has made many enemies. She is naively puzzled at this.
Why is she hated? she asks. She has brought victory, she
has corrected everybody's stupidities, and she has made
Charles king. Furthermore, she has asked nothing for
herself.

Dunois is both amused and moved by Joan's innocence.
He explains that stupid people are not grateful when
somebody shows them how stupid they are. Military
men do not like their blunders revealed. Politicians do not
enjoy losing their influence. Archbishops do not like to be
pushed from their eminence, even by saints.

Shaw is exemplifying the analysis of Joan in the early

sections of the Preface. She is undoubtedly brilliant. But she is also young and ignorant. She has not learned the necessity of tact. She thinks it is enough to show people what is right; then they will be grateful. But people hate anyone who says to them: "You are behaving stupidly. Let me show you what you should do."

To Dunois, Joan reveals that she hears her voices in the echoes of the church chimes. At each quarter, she hears a different message; at the hour, she sometimes hears the saints speaking to her.

Dunois is gentle, but he does not have much sympathy when Joan tells him of her voices. He believes she hears whatever she wishes to imagine in the bells. He points out that Joan always has sensible reasons for what she does, though she claims that she is only doing what the saints tell her to. Dunois is expressing Shaw's analysis of Joan's voices—that they are her own brilliant insights embodied in voices by her vivid imagination.

Charles enters with La Hire and Bluebeard. He is complaining irritably that the robes and crown for the coronation were uncomfortably heavy and the holy oil was rancid. Joan tells the king she is going home to her father's farm. He cannot hide his pleasure at the news.

COMMENT: Charles has reverted back to his natural character, now that the glamor of the Maid's inspiration has worn off. He is again revealed as a pettish, small-minded man who wants to do everything the easiest way, without inconvenience. The triumph of his coronation does not matter to him next to the fact that he found it physically uncomfortable. He is delighted at the idea of being rid of Joan. She is always forcing him on to make further efforts, when he wants to sit back and take it easy. Speed and daring are foreign to his nature. Now she is urging him to try to take Paris, while he wants to make a treaty with the rebel Duke of Burgundy.

The Archbishop joins them. Joan directs him to tell the king that God commands him to keep on fighting. The Archbishop reproaches Joan for her pride; he says that her earlier humility has been lost. La Hire backs Joan's idea of attacking Paris, but Dunois is against it. Dunois says Joan has daring, but not generalship. Joan in turn reproaches Dunois; she states that his knights play at war instead of fighting to the death.

COMMENT: Like Charles, the Archbishop is finding prolonged association with Joan irritating. He does not feel his position as an exalted churchman is sufficiently respected when Joan gives him a message from God to deliver to the king. He prophesies that her pride will bring her to a fall, and it seems as though he takes a certain pleasure in the prospect.

Even Dunois, who is sincerely attached to her, is not pleased when she overlooks all he did to make her successes possible. Joan led the troops to victory, but Dunois had to supply the troops and feed them. Dunois believes that God has helped Joan, but he does not believe she "has God in her pocket." If they try to take Paris without sufficient men and sufficient preparation, they are bound to fail.

Only La Hire supports Joan unreservedly, though even he remarks that when she goes home, he will be able to swear whenever he likes.

Joan has no respect for Dunois' cautious strategy because it is based on the use of armored knights in battle. These unwieldly fighters cannot even get up off the ground if they are knocked down from their horses, and they are interested in ransom, not victory. Joan points out that gunpowder makes them useless. The common people know how to fight; they put their lives into God's hand and continue to the death. It is on such fighting that strategy must be based.

In all this, Joan shows that she is a brilliant military strategist centuries ahead of her time. As Shaw says in the Preface, Joan's ideas on war were much like Napoleon's, almost four centuries later. Shaw makes Joan a very conscious critic of medieval warfare, in line with his dramatic method of having characters explain clearly things which in real life they would only grasp instinctively or not at all.

Dunois reveals that Warwick is offering to pay sixteen thousand pounds to anyone who captures Joan. In turn they explain why they will not help her if she is captured—Dunois because she will no longer be useful to him, Charles because he cannot spare any money, and the Archbishop because she is proud and disobedient. Aware that she is completely alone, Joan passes into the street as the scene ends.

COMMENT: Note that this final section of Scene V is very formal in its arrangement. Each of Joan's associates steps forth in turn to tell her that she must do without his aid. The effect is almost operatic—as though the three men were performing a trio. The tone of each solo varies—for Dunois has affection for Joan, while Charles and the Archbishop do not care about her. Yet the end result is the same. Dunois regretfully announces that when Joan is captured and imprisoned, she will become a mere human, no longer an invulnerable heavenly being who can inspire the army. Therefore he cannot risk a single soldier's life to save her, even though he would gladly give his own for her sake.

Charles states irritably that he has no money for ransom. The coronation has taken every cent he could borrow, and the coronation, he says to his rescuer angrily, "is all your fault." This is one of the finest lines in the play. With painful irony, it shows what rewards a great man or woman can expect from lesser human beings.

The Archbishop's angry rejection of Joan is based on hurt pride. She does not treat him with the great reverence he expects. Yet, though he may have unworthy personal reasons, he does accurately point out the reason why the Church will condemn Joan. She has refused the Church's counsel, not only that of the Archbishop.

Joan is thunderstruck at the notion that she could be considered a witch. But even when the Archbishop tells her this, she insists on the truth of her voices. She digests what they all have said to her and at last makes her own speech. She realizes her loneliness, but compares it to the loneliness of France and the loneliness of God. Proudly she accepts it. She even accepts the possibility that she may go to the fire; if it happens, she knows she will live in the hearts of the people forever. She goes out alone, which makes the scene balanced and complete, for at the beginning, she was alone in prayer, and now she is again alone with God.

A perfect conclusion is created as the others react to her magnificence. Bluebeard refers to her haughtily as "impossible." And poor foolish Charles, longing for his peace and his comfort, wishes once more that she would go home. Only La Hire is still loyal.

SCENE VI

COMMENT:	The play *Saint Joan* is constructed with great artistry. The first three scenes recount with rising splendor Joan's coming and triumph. With the fourth scene, Joan's doom begins. The mood changes. Warwick and Cauchon discuss her destruction. In Scene V, her own followers prove to be no less her enemies than the English themselves. Scene VI, the trial scene, the longest, weightiest, richest scene in the play, completes her destruction.

In this scene, Shaw stays very close to history. Depending on the records of Joan's trial edited by Jules Quicherat and published in 1841, the playwright often uses Joan's own words in the dialogue. He has merely tightened and condensed the material to increase its dramatic value. His only major addition is the behavior of Chaplain de Stogumber at the end of the play. Shaw has created in the scene a combination of intellectual stimulation and powerful emotional force which has seldom been equaled in English drama.

The scene is the castle at Rouen, on May 30, 1431. A great
stone hall is ready for Joan's trial. Warwick enters the empty
room, followed shortly by Cauchon and two other churchmen.
These are the Dominican monk, Brother John Le Maitre, who
represents the Holy Inquisition, and Canon D'Estivet, who
is acting as Promoter (prosecutor). Courteously, but with
a hint of threat, Warwick asks why it is taking so long to
try the Maid. She has been a prisoner for nine months and
in Cauchon's hands for three months. Cauchon replies that
they are ready to begin.

> **COMMENT:** This opening serves in part to bring the
> audience or reader up to date on events since the last
> scene. From Warwick's remarks, it is clear that Joan did
> indeed attack the city of Compiègne and did suffer im-
> prisonment by the Burgundians, just as Lunois predicted
> in Scene V. Now the English have bought her and turned
> her over to Cauchon for trial.
>
> We also learn about the slowness and care of the
> Church's proceedings against Joan. There have been
> eleven weeks of preliminary questioning. Joan has under-
> gone fifteen pretrial examinations. Her case is to be
> judged by Cauchon and Le Maitre, who is a specialist
> on the subject of heresy, as well as by a number of other
> clergymen.
>
> **A NOTE ON THE INQUISITION.** Le Maitre is a repre-
> sentative of the Inquisition. This was an organization set
> up in 1233. At that time, certain Dominican monks were
> given power by the Pope to investigate heresy. The prac-
> tice of the Inquisitors was to give a light penance to those
> who confessed their heresy. Those who did not recant,
> however, were brought to trial and, if found guilty, con-
> demned to penance, fines, imprisonment, or death at the
> stake. However, the Inquisitors preferred to avoid trials
> and secure a confession and the heretic's return to the
> church whenever possible.
>
> This should not be confused with the notorious Spanish
> Inquisition, which came into existence much later. It was

founded by King Ferdinand and Queen Isabella (the
sponsors of Columbus) in 1478 and was used mainly as a
method of political persecution. Its proceedings were
much more cruel than those of the medieval Inquisition.
It also used the death penalty more frequently.

The antagonism between Warwick and Cauchon, only
hinted at in Scene IV, becomes clearly developed here.
Warwick virtually orders Cauchon to stop delaying and
send the girl to the stake. There can be no question of
saving her. Her death is politically necessary. Cauchon
insists sternly that Joan shall have a fair trial. She shall
go free if the court releases her. The Church is not to be
used as a political convenience by the English.

The Inquisitor stops the quarrel by revealing that Joan
is sure to condemn herself. Each time she speaks she con-
victs herself. Warwick then gives cynical approval to their
efforts: they should certainly try to save her, as long as
it will do no good.

Warwick leaves the hall so that the trial can begin. The "asses-
sors" (assisting clergy) enter. Chaplain de Stogumber is among
them. He and his friend Master de Courcelles, Canon of Paris,
object to the proceedings: their indictment (document listing
accusations) of Joan had sixty-four charges against her; they
have now been reduced to twelve. De Courcelles is also concerned because nobody is taking seriously the accusation that
Joan stole a horse from the Bishop of Senlis. The Inquisitor
politely suggests that they had better concentrate on the issue
of heresy.

COMMENT: Courcelles is a fitting companion to Stogumber. They have about the same amount of intelligence,
which is not much. However, while Stogumber is so loyal
to things English that his intellect does not work at all
when English interests are involved, Courcelles is stupid
in a different way. He is the man who can never keep
his mind on the main issue. He is constantly sidetracked
by unimportant points. He cannot cope with logic. The
Inquisitor cannot make it clear to him that if Joan is

burned for heresy it will not really matter whether she
is also convicted of stealing the Bishop's horse.

Courcelles and Stogumber provide a small degree of
comic relief in this touching and terrible trial scene.
Notice that the humor they create still has a definite connection with the material of the scene. The scene depicts
Joan's trial. These two foolish men are funny because
they cannot comprehend what the trial is about.

Brother Martin Ladvenu, a young Dominican friar, asks
whether Joan's heresy is really harmful. Is it not a result of
her ignorance and innocence? The Inquisitor responds with a
solemn explanation about the dangers of heresy.

COMMENT: The Inquisitor's speech is the longest, and
some feel the best, in the play. It takes about seven
minutes to deliver on the stage. From it we receive a
full explanation of the dangers of heresy. The Inquisitor's
work is shown in the most favorable light possible.

To summarize, the speech states that most heretics are
sincerely pious people who begin by seeming better than
others. But when they do things outside the teachings
of the Church, even with the best of intentions, they stir
up other people to more wicked disobedience. The heretic
woman wears man's clothes; her followers may refuse
to wear any clothes at all. So it is with Joan. She is a
pious, humble girl. But her inspiration is from the devil.
And she may lure many others away from the teachings
of the Church. The court must not be angry with her.
Nor must it be misled by pity. It must administer justice
with mercy.

The Inquisitor's speech is both responsible and intelligent.
It is miles away from the bigoted stupidity of Stogumber
and Courcelles. It has the effect of lifting the trial from
melodrama to tragedy. That is, we do not see a wicked
villain persecuting an innocent heroine; that is what we
call melodrama. Instead, we see a kind and thoughtful
man doing what he believes is the right thing. Yet,

though his thoughts are worthy of our respectful attention, he happens to be prosecuting a genius and a saint. This terrible outcome, when both sides are obeying their consciences and doing what they must, is tragic. It makes us aware of the inevitability of human error and human suffering.

Cauchon adds a few words about the particular heresy of "Protestantism." The trial is ready to begin. Joan is brought in. She complains about being held in English hands, rather than by the Church; also, she hates being chained by her ankles to a log of wood. She is impatient with the questions put to her by D'Estivet. She finds them foolish and shows it.

> **COMMENT:** Joan has been through a great ordeal. In her black suit (a page's costume, not a woman's), she looks pale and strained. But she still has her courage. Spiritedly, she objects to being with Warwick's soldiers day and night. Joan is strong and active, a country girl used to freedom of movement. Being chained by her ankles to a log must be particularly difficult for her to endure. She has a lively discussion with her captors about it. Courcelles points out that she jumped from a tower sixty feet high in an effort to escape and did not die; this proves she must be a witch. She replies that the tower was not sixty feet high when she jumped from it; it has been getting higher every time it has been mentioned. In other words, the story has been steadily exaggerated, until it has become fantastic.
>
> Joan also shows her spirit in her words to D'Estivet, her prosecutor. According to him, Joan's effort to escape was heresy, for she was trying to desert the Church. Joan calls this feeble argument "nonsense."
>
> To summarize, before her trial begins, Joan is still supplied with vital strength. Her faith in her voices supports her, making her able to defend herself against her captors.

Now the Inquisitor calls for a formal opening to the proceedings. He asks Joan to swear to tell the whole truth. Joan

objects that she cannot tell the whole truth: God does not
permit it. She is threatened with torture. The Inquisitor,
Cauchon, and Ladvenu are unwilling to use it. Courcelles
urges its use because it is always done.

COMMENT: This illustrates the exceptional mercy and
caution of Joan's judges. They are unwilling to employ
torture unless it is absolutely necessary. Torture is used
to extract a confession, and since Joan freely makes
statements that convict her of heresy, torture is not re-
quired. Only Courcelles insists on it—not because he is
cruel, or even because he has any idea of what it may
accomplish. His reason is only that torture is customary,
provoking Joan to observe accurately that he is "a rare
noodle" (fool).

Historically, Shaw is correct. Joan was not tortured, a
mercy remarked upon by virtually all those who have
studied or commented on the trial.

Cauchon now proceeds to the heart of the matter. Will Joan
accept the judgment of the Church concerning her actions and
especially her visions? The Inquisitor and Ladvenu also urge
her to do so. Her answer is always the same: she accepts the
judgment of the Church in all matters except those that concern her visions and her orders from God. She will not deny
these, no matter who tells her to. In the midst of this vital
dispute, Courcelles brings up the matter of the Bishop's horse,
causing Cauchon to lose his temper.

COMMENT: As Cauchon, the Inquisitor, and Ladvenu
struggle and plead with Joan to save her life and her soul,
we see an example of Shaw's special dramatic gifts. The
material of the scene is highly abstract: it involves the
difference between the views of the Church and of the
inspired individual. The Church insists upon the necessity
of judging Joan's visions, for the Church guides the individual soul to God. But Joan feels she has been directly
inspired, and she dares not deny that inspiration.

This intellectual material is presented in vividly personal

terms which make it truly dramatic. The characters are strongly distinguished from one another. Cauchon is dedicated and conscientious; the Inquisitor is kind; Ladvenu shows a sensitive pity for Joan; Joan herself holds steadily to the things she has lived by. With powerful effect, Shaw has her say something which the real Joan is reported to have said at her trial, about being in a state of grace: "If I am not, may God bring me to it; if I am, may God keep me in it."

Courcelles' ridiculous interruption is all the more effective because it comes after this beautiful remark. It provides a striking change of pace, and yet it helps clarify the discussion still further. When Cauchon becomes furiously angry, the play becomes far more personal and concrete. Nevertheless the point of the discussion is not lost, for Cauchon's outburst makes the importance of what he has been trying to do very clear. If he were not wholeheartedly concerned over Joan's heresy and possible conviction, he would not be so enraged at Courcelles.

D'Estivet charges Joan with associating with evil spirits and dressing as a man. Joan denies that the spirits are evil. She defends wearing male clothing: if she dressed as a woman among soldiers, what would become of her? The male clothing is a protection. When they accuse her of pride, she is honestly puzzled. She does not understand them.

COMMENT: Joan of course denies that her visions are evil spirits. They are Saint Catherine, Saint Margaret, and Michael the Archangel. With his genius for picking out what is unimportant, Courcelles asks whether Michael appears to her naked. Joan makes a famous response to this, taken exactly from the records of the real trial. She asks whether Courcelles thinks God cannot afford clothes for him.

Shaw points out in the Preface that Joan's voices never told her to do anything that was not sensible. She could always give a logical reason for any command she received. Shaw is supporting his interpretation of Joan's

voices—that they were her own genius, presented in
vivid form by her imagination. We have an example of
this when Shaw has Joan defend the wearing of men's
clothes, which is so shocking to her judges. The order
to wear the clothes comes from Saint Catherine, but Joan
explains that when she wears soldiers' clothes, the men
think of her as a soldier, not as a woman. In other words,
she has a good reason for her action.

Ladvenu reproaches Joan for her pride; she will not listen
to the wisdom of the Church. Joan really does not know
what he is talking about. She is not proud. She is doing
what God has told her. We see here that she is so naive
that she cannot comprehend the nature of the charge
against her. Later, after Joan has been taken away to her
death, the Inquisitor states that she never understood a
word they said to her; she suffers because of her ignorance.

Ladvenu tries to make Joan understand how near death is to
her. He has the Executioner describe the stake which is waiting
in the marketplace for the moment when she has been excommunicated. Desperate, she agrees to recant. Stogumber
is furious at her possible escape from the fire.

COMMENT: The Executioner is a quiet, frightening
figure. He answers Ladvenu's questions in a few words,
without emotion. This makes the stake waiting outside
seem all the more horrible. Joan's shock at the business-
like arrangements, all ready and waiting, is reflected in
the audience.

Joan states that her voices have promised that she will
not burn. The real Joan did make this statement. Shaw
feels that this confirms his idea that Joan's voices were
simply reflections of her own thoughts. She was sure that
Dunois and his army would save her, and so she heard
her voices promise her rescue.

Joan's recantation is beautifully poignant. The recantation
is a frightful step for Joan. She makes it from the depths
of terror and despair. It involves giving up the most sacred

and cherished part of her life. Her instinctive wish to live, as powerful as that of an animal, drives her to do it.

She cannot write her name. Ladvenu guides her hand to form the letters; then she makes her mark on the paper. This reminds us of her youth and ignorance and increases the pathos of the scene.

Stogumber sees the possibility slowly growing that Joan will escape. He is as furious as some wild animal deprived of food. He abuses the court and the French, swearing that the witch will burn, no matter what their verdict.

The Inquisitor handles him as easily as if he were a child in a tantrum. When told to sit down, he stands. The Inquisitor simply suggests that he keep standing; he then sits down at once.

After Joan signs the recantation, the Inquisitor frees her from the danger of excommunication. But he sentences her to imprisonment for life. When Joan hears this, she tears up the paper she has signed. She would rather die than live in prison.

COMMENT: In real life, Joan did not go back on her recantation until several days after she made it. We can only guess at her reason for doing so. Shaw assumes that she would not face life in prison and virtually killed herself by refusing to honor the document she had signed. For purposes of the play, he has her tear up the paper as soon as she hears the sentence of imprisonment.

Joan's beautiful speech, in which she praises the beauties of her simple free country life, which she cannot do without, is deeply moving. As in most of Joan's speeches, the language is a combination of sensitivity and uneducated simplicity. The sentiments expressed seem to reflect Shaw's great horror of imprisonment, which he regarded as more cruel than torture or death.

After Joan's defiance, Cauchon and the Inquisitor excom-

municate her. Joan is taken outside to her execution, with
Stogumber eagerly assisting the soldiers. Ladvenu goes to
comfort Joan. All follow, except Cauchon and the Inquisitor.
Cauchon is disgusted at the rushed, irregular proceedings, but
the Inquisitor prevents him from interfering. Warwick enters.
His dislike for Cauchon becomes very clear. The churchmen
leave.

COMMENT: The sentence against Joan is solemnly
spoken by the Inquisitor and Cauchon. They alternate, as
though to share the responsibility of the words they are
saying. The disorganized rushing of Joan to the fire is in
contrast to their formal solemnity. Stogumber's eagerness
to burn the girl is indecent. It creates revulsion on the
part of the audience.

The Inquisitor shows that he is politically shrewd. We
have seen him so far only as a dedicated churchman; this
exhibition of worldly wisdom on his part is something of a
shock. When Cauchon wants to halt the irregular execution, he points out that the sooner it is over, the better
for Joan—and it may someday be useful to have something
to blame the English for.

The Inquisitor also shows the extent of his wisdom when
he mentions that of course Joan was innocent. That is,
she did not understand what she was accused of. This
does not make it less necessary to kill her (the heretic
often acts in ignorance) but it does sadden the man who
has helped sentence her to death.

Warwick enters the courtroom while the execution is
under way. He cannot look upon the burning of Joan,
though he cynically arranged it as a political convenience.
Cauchon and the Inquisitor see the affair through; they
go out to the courtyard, to be witnesses to Joan's death.
After an exchange of insulting remarks between Cauchon
and Warwick, the Englishman is left alone in the courtroom.

In a moment, Stogumber enters from the courtyard, howling

and sobbing. The reality of the burning was so dreadful that it has caused his emotional collapse. He is hysterical with pity and remorse.

COMMENT: Stogumber's reaction is one of Shaw's most brilliant devices. In no other way could the dreadfulness of Joan's death be so powerfully brought home to the audience without showing any physical horror. The man who could not wait to see that the "witch" was burned has found her suffering and death unbearable.

The incident also conveys a striking characterization of Stogumber, as well as a philosophical comment. We understand at this point that Stogumber is not cruel or bloodthirsty, as we may have thought in earlier scenes. He is a man of simple mind who can only grasp one idea at a time. He is so concerned with the military failure of the English that he does not have room for any other thought. His imagination does not function. He clamors for Joan's death because she has defeated the English. It is not until he sees and smells her dying that he understands what he has been clamoring for.

Shaw seems to be saying that it is not the wicked people that do the greatest mischief; it is the stupid people with no imagination that cause the worst damage.

Ladvenu enters. He tells how he held a cross for Joan to see, and how she warned him away because he might be burned. He is convinced that she is now with God. Stogumber rushes out wildly. Ladvenu follows to prevent him from harming himself.

The executioner comes to report to Warwick. Only Joan's heart would not burn. It is at the bottom of the river. He assures Warwick that he has heard the last of her. Warwick is not so sure.

COMMENT: Ladvenu appears here as the prophet of Joan's glory. The nobility of her death has converted him. The sympathy he showed for her during the trial has been turned into active belief in her heavenly inspiration. He states that her death is not an end but a beginning. This is Warwick's first evidence that he has failed to destroy Joan. When the Executioner assures him that he will hear no more of her, Warwick remembers Ladvenu's words and says thoughtfully, "I wonder."

The Executioner is again a forbidding figure as he describes Joan's death. He chills us the more because he is so workmanlike, a craftsman describing the performance of an efficient job. Proudly, he describes his profession as a highly skilled mystery. "Mystery" is an old word for "craft" or "skill."

THE EPILOGUE

GENERAL COMMENT: This is the scene of *Saint Joan* that has always aroused the liveliest debate. Those who do not care for it do not necessarily dislike the scene itself; indeed, many admire its profound thought and its witty expression. But they feel it descends from the high mood of tragic pity which is created by the conclusion of Scene VI. Warwick's slight discomfort, Stogumber's distraction, and Ladvenu's kindled devotion combine to end the play magnificently. We have the sense that Joan's death is a tragic occurrence out of which moral change will grow—for Joan was a person who moved all that came near her.

Yet the main idea behind the play is that the genius is a human being whose insights are far ahead of those of most other people; therefore the behavior of the genius will be puzzling and disturbing to most people. Most human beings, though they may be temporarily inspired by the genius, will eventually find that he makes them uncomfortable. They will be very glad to be rid of him when he is taken away from them. This idea is suggested in the play, especially in the fifth scene. But it is developed with the greatest wit and power in the Epilogue. For this reason, some critics regard the Epilogue as the very center of the play, absolutely indispensable. Shaw himself stated amiably but definitely in the Preface that the play would not be complete without the Epilogue. (See section of Preface entitled "The Epilogue," with Comment, above.)

The scene is the bedroom of King Charles the Seventh, formerly the Dauphin. It is June, 1456, twenty-five years after Joan's execution. Charles is in bed; outside, there is a thunderstorm. Ladvenu enters to announce that an inquiry has put aside the verdict at her trial and justified her.

Joan appears. It becomes evident that Charles is dreaming. In turn, others appear—Cauchon, Dunois, Stogumber, the Executioner, Warwick, the Archbishop, and the Inquisitor. Cauchon, dead, is bitterly resentful of the way his reputation has been slandered, because of his part in Joan's trial. Stogumber is very infirm, and his mind has been permanently affected by the burning of Joan.

A strange soldier also appears. He has a day off from Hell every year because he tied two sticks together and gave them to the Maid at the stake.

The last stranger is an official from the year 1920, come to announce Joan's sainthood. All kneel and praise her. But when she asks whether she should come back to life, all refuse and leave her. The soldier from Hell is the last person to go. Joan drops to her knees and asks God when the earth will be ready for its saints.

COMMENT: As it becomes evident that some time has passed since the last scene, the audience watches with great interest to find out what has happened to the characters. Charles seems much the same as before, though he later tells Joan that he has learned physical courage and now leads his armies in battle. Joan is almost unchanged. She is, as she says, hardly even a ghost—only the content of a dream. She speaks in the same way: the King is still "Charlie" to her. But she is mellower. With the passage of time, she has come to accept and under-

stand all that has happened. There is a great calm about
her.

Ladvenu is like a man possessed. He carries the cross
that he held for Joan to see when she was dying. Charles
has heard that he has "a bee in his bonnet" about the
Maid. That is, the justification of Joan has become the
main purpose of his life. He announces Joan's triumph in
solemn tones. Also, he embodies an important paradox
of the play in his speech. That is, Joan's original trial
was fair and merciful, but the verdict was a lie and the
sentence was a horror. The inquiry was a farce, full of
bribery and false testimony. Yet the conclusion of it was
a triumph of truth.

Of the others, Dunois and Warwick are most obviously
the same and Stogumber is the most sadly changed.
Dunois shows the same combination of warmheartedness
and practicality. Warwick has the same suave manner,
and the same lack of moral sense. He apologizes courteously to Joan for the burning, as if it were a small lapse of
manners on his part. He also remarks that politically it
was a very bad mistake. Joan meant even more to France
after her death than before.

Poor John de Stogumber, now white-haired and bent, is
the rector of a little country village. His mind dwells dis-
connectedly on the terrible death of Joan. When he saw
what cruelty was really like, he says, his soul was saved.
Disgustedly Cauchon remarks that Christ's sufferings must
be constantly repeated for those who have no imagination.

The soldier is a fine invention by Shaw. His coming is
heralded by a doggerel march the men made up during
the war. He does not recognize Joan as the girl to whom
he gave the crudely made cross; to him, one girl is pretty
much like another. And he is a little defensive about his
one good action, as though he expects everyone to make
fun of him for it.

There is an amusing small piece of dialogue between this

soldier and Charles. When Charles asks him what Hell is like, he replies: "You won't find it so bad, sir." Apparently, his experience in Hell has led him to assume that kings end up there as a matter of course.

The soldier's description of Hell is briefly reminiscent of the elaborate discussion in *Man and Superman;* in this latter play, Hell is characterized as the place for irresponsible people who enjoy wasting time and living with illusions. Here, the soldier describes it as a jolly place where you always feel as if you were drunk.

When the official representative from 1920 arrives with tail coat and high hat, he evokes loud laughter from everybody, much to his indignation. They laugh at his "fancy dress"; he is just as sure that they are in ridiculous costumes. Dunois sensibly points out that all dress is fancy dress except our skins.

The joking fades away as, in a moment of formal solemnity, each of those present falls on his knees before Joan and praises her. But Joan wisely responds that she is in difficulties if all men praise her. She asks if she should rise from the dead and return to life. Without exception, those who have known her are dismayed by the idea. Their reasons range from the exalted (Cauchon points out that Joan is still dangerous because most men cannot distinguish between the saint and the heretic) to the commonplace (the executioner worries about what will happen to his income if those whom he has killed cannot be trusted to stay dead).

Only the soldier is ready to stay with Joan. But midnight strikes, and he is forced to return to Hell. Alone, Joan prays the prayer of the genius-saint (in the play and its Preface Shaw uses the terms almost synonymously)— when will the world be ready for her? How long will she be rejected by the rest of mankind? In this final moment, both beautiful and ironic, Shaw brings home to us with great power his idea that we cannot forgive or welcome the great ones among us.

CHARACTER ANALYSES

JOAN: As Shaw describes her, Joan is a genius, especially in military affairs, with a vivid imagination and a strong will. Her brilliant ideas, such as the relief of Orléans and the crowing of Charles at Rheims, come to her in auditory form. She hears voices telling her what to do, voices which she identifies as Saint Catherine, Saint Margaret, and the Archangel Michael. Once inspired in this way, Joan lets nothing and nobody stand in her way. She overwhelms her own family, Baudricourt, the Dauphin, and Dunois.

Joan's entire interest is concentrated in traditionally masculine affairs. She has no interest in woman's work, though she has been trained to spin and weave like any well-brought-up girl of her class.

However, Joan is handicapped by her own extraordinary nature. She cannot understand why anyone should resent her. She is not petty herself, and so she does not comprehend this trait in others. She does not understand how people hate to have their stupidity shown up, to other people and especially to themselves. She proceeds grandly, with complete tactlessness, to tell all her associates what they are doing wrong and how they should do it right. Of course, they hate this, even though they may benefit from it.

Joan's language is a fine reflection of herself. On the one hand it shows her simple country origins, for it is rough and unlearned; but on the other hand, it sometimes glows with poetic delicacy and rare insight. It is full of the affection Joan feels for all of God's creatures.

Her religion is the great joy of her life. She is overwhelmed with ecstatic piety when she first sees a real live Archbishop, even though he happens to be a rather worldly churchman. Shrewdly, he observes that she is in love with religion. Later, Dunois points out that she is in love with war. These are, in fact, the two great loves of Joan's existence.

To summarize, Joan is a genius (or saint) of intellectual

genius, powerful will, and unselfish dedication. But she suffers from ignorance and tactlessness. Her concerns are war and religion.

THE DAUPHIN (LATER KING CHARLES VII):   Charles is a small-minded man. He composes a sort of summation of himself in the Epilogue when he describes himself as a good fellow in his own little way. Charles has no desire to remake the world into a better place. He is physically and morally lazy; if left to himself, he drifts along, changing nothing, enjoying his comfort, taking things as they come. It is astonishing that Joan is able to fill a man like this with fire and purpose. Of course, this effect is only temporary. Joan becomes a burden to Charles. He is annoyed because his coronation has cost him money he can ill afford; he loses sight of the fact that it strengthens his position immeasurably. Soon he is wishing she would go home.

Charles is physically weak. He is not naturally equipped to be a fifteenth-century fighting man. He cannot carry the armor and he cannot handle a heavy sword. This makes him less disposed than ever to act as a strong leader. He is also intelligent enough to see that much of the fighting that goes on is useless, since it accomplishes nothing that could not be done by peaceful means. But Joan is clear-sighted enough to realize that there are times when one must fight.

To summarize, Charles is a kindly, rather intelligent man. But he is also lazy and selfish. Loyalty and gratitude are not among his virtues. He owes his crown to Joan, but he lets her be burned without making any effort on her behalf.

PETER CAUCHON, BISHOP OF BEAUVAIS: In the official view of the Church inquiry of 1456, Cauchon was an evil, dishonest man. He was excommunicated; his dead body was dug up and thrown into the sewer. But Shaw shows him as a man of exceptional conscience and integrity. He is the unrelenting enemy of heresy, especially that heresy which puts individual judgment against the wisdom of the Church. But, in spite of this, he is not Joan's enemy. He has her treated with consideration. He will not permit her to be tortured. He strives with all his might to reclaim Joan from the mortal sin into which he believes she has fallen. His final sentence on her is pronounced with regret.

Shaw indicates in the Preface that he has exaggerated Cauchon's virtue and understanding for the sake of presenting him in a clear and dramatic manner.

EARL OF WARWICK: There is no attractive Englishman in this play. Warwick is far from appealing. His diplomatic courtesy conceals a cold heart. He has no conscience. A hideous action like the burning of Joan does not trouble him, as long as he can explain it as a political necessity. In the Epilogue, he apologizes to Joan with trivial politeness, as though he has been slightly rude to her instead of burning her alive.

Like Cauchon, Warwick has more intelligence and self-understanding than he probably did in real life.

CHAPLAIN DE STOGUMBER: This second important Englishman in the play represents the naive patriot, in contrast to Warwick, the sophisticated diplomat. He is a satire on all Englishmen of this type, modern as well as medieval.

In the early part of the play, the Chaplain is Joan's deadly enemy. The English have lost battles because of her. It is not natural or proper for the English to lose battles; therefore the girl must be a witch. Cauchon distinguishes between a witch and a heretic, but Stogumber is not interested in that. The important thing is that she must be burned. He does not worry about what exactly she is to be burned for.

Stogumber is eager for Joan's execution throughout her trial. When she recants temporarily, he creates a noisy disturbance in his fear lest she escape the fire. Eagerly, he helps the soldiers take her out to the courtyard and the stake.

Within a few minutes, he is back in the courtroom, with an agony in his soul that will last all his life. He has seen the burning. Now for the first time he knows what it is like. He understands what he has done. He is not really a monstrously cruel man. He is a foolish man without imagination. He is one of those who will never understand the harm he does unless he sees it before his eyes.

DUNOIS, THE BASTARD OF ORLEANS: In Dunois, there is a mixture of faith and practicality. He becomes convinced that Joan is sent from God when the wind changes at Orléans. His appreciation and affection for Joan do not waver from that time on. But Dunois is an experienced military commander. He knows that Joan does not understand much about strategy when she first comes to him. She is brave, but she runs head on into danger unless Dunois stops her and explains what is possible and why. Even in the period of Joan's greatest success, Dunois supplies troops for her to lead, and he sees that those troops are fed and armed. He tells her she will run into trouble at Compiègne, and she does. Dunois' solid practical ability supports Joan throughout her career. His generous nature is unstained by jealousy of the "little saint" who has taken over his command—and his fame.

However, the strong intelligence of Dunois prevents him from following Joan to disaster. Kindly but firmly, he warns her that if she gets herself captured at Compiègne, she will be of no military use to him. The soldiers will no longer believe that she cannot be taken by the enemy. They will no longer follow her fearlessly. Therefore, though his warm feeling for the marvelous country girl has not changed, he will not sacrifice the lives of his men to save her.

Also, Dunois has little confidence in Joan's voices. When Joan tells him that she hears the saints speaking in the church bells, he does not make fun of her, but he does tell her gently that she hears whatever she wants to hear.

In short, Dunois is a realistic though kind-natured person, who feels admiration for Joan but recognizes her limitations.

ROBERT DE BAUDRICOURT: Only the first scene of the play features Robert de Baudricourt. He is sketched briefly but effectively. He is one of those people who do not feel sure of themselves and who try to conceal this from the world with an air of great assurance. The more uncertain he feels, the more noisily assertive he becomes. His fierce bluster has no effect on Joan at all. On the contrary, her cheerful confidence makes him uneasy. When the unexcitable Squire de Poulengey expresses faith in Joan, his uneasiness becomes obvious. At last, his opposition crumbles entirely, and he sends Joan to the Dauphin, very unhappy at having to accept the responsibility on his own shoulders.

Baudricourt does not have much intelligence (in fact, one of his colleagues refers to him as a blazing ass). The trivial coincidence of the hens beginning to lay eggs after he does what Joan wants him to convinces him that she came from God. The clearly unique nature of the girl herself does not succeed in doing this.

THE ARCHBISHOP OF RHEIMS: This is a shrewd, worldly man who has made his career in the Church. His explanation of miracles shows us what kind of man he is. He tells La Trémouille that a miracle is an event which creates faith. Even if it is contrived by human beings for that purpose it is still a miracle. In other words, he is far more concerned with what is useful than with what is true.

There is still enough sensibility concealed in the Archbishop to make him a little ashamed when Joan exhibits naive reverence toward him as an incarnation of the Church's glory. But he is touched by her deep piety only for a short time. Soon he becomes irritated at Joan's pride and self-sufficiency. He is one of those whom Joan touches but does not change.

DUC DE LA TREMOUILLE: He is a rough military commander with an understanding of power but not book learning. The Archbishop's explanation of miracles confuses his blunt intelligence. He has no respect for the Dauphin, for the Dauphin is opposite to him in all his traits. He lets the Dauphin see plainly how he feels. He cannot read very easily, but this does not bother him. He would far rather be his own strong and ignorant self than the insignificant, intelligent Dauphin.

We are left with an impression of physical strength and violent temper.

GILLES DE RAIS: We observe him as a dashing young courtier who does not hesitate to make rather cruel fun of the Dauphin. We find him piquantly interesting mainly because we know that he will have a notorious future as a child-murderer (which will make the name "Bluebeard" famous) and a violent, shameful death.

CAPTAIN LA HIRE: This soldier is famous for his bad language until his life is touched by Joan. He stops swearing (or tries to), convinced that Joan prophesied the death of another foul-mouthed fellow like himself, who then drowned. To the end, he is responsive to Joan's fiery eloquence; but occasionally he thinks wistfully that it would be nice if Joan would go home, so that he could swear again.

THE INQUISITOR: This Dominican monk is a member of the Holy Inquisition, whose business it is to investigate and get rid of heresy. Shaw gets a paradoxical effectiveness by making a member of the Inquisition into a mild, scholarly, conscientious old gentleman. To most people, the term "Inquisition" brings to mind pictures of relentless persecutions and cruel tortures. This man is very different. He does his work only because he is convinced that to leave it undone is extremely dangerous. In the longest speech in the play, he explains the wickedness and destruction that follow heresy. Therefore, he is gentle to Joan as he carries out his duty. He is relentless only to what he sees as her sin.

COURCELLES: Courcelles, the Canon of Paris, is the ally of Chaplain de Stogumber at the trial. He does not have Stogumber's emotional patriotism to excuse him. He is merely a brainless man with a lot of determination. He has only the dimmest understanding of what is going on. Each time he interrupts the proceedings, he hurts rather than helps his own side. He is angry when the sixty-four counts of the original indictment, many of them unimportant or silly, are reduced to twelve by the Inquisitor. While the mighty issue of heresy is being investigated, his mind is wholly taken up with the alleged theft

of the Bishop of Senlis' horse. And he is most anxious for Joan
to be tortured, not because he likes torture, but because it is
always done. His absurdities provide a light touch in the
somber trial scene.

Joan calls Courcelles a "rare noodle." He is indignant, but
the audience recognizes it as a just evaluation.

BROTHER MARTIN LADVENU: At the trial, Ladvenu is seen as
a Dominican monk who shows unusual sensitivity to Joan's
pitiful youth and innocence. He does all that he can to save the
girl from death. It is he who makes the executioner describe
the stake waiting for Joan outside the courtroom. This makes
Joan realize for the first time the nearness of death and leads
to her recantation. Ladvenu writes it for her and guides her
hand in the signature. When she is finally sentenced, he covers
his face with his hands in an involuntary gesture of grief.

After the execution, Ladvenue returns with the tale of how
Joan sent him away from her for fear he would be burned.
He is converted; now he is sure that not a heretic, but a child
of God has been among them.

The Epilogue shows Ladvenu, still carrying the cross he held
for Joan to look on as she died, now completely dedicated to
Joan's memory. The only purpose of his life is to justify her.
Ladvenu is one of those whose life was briefly touched by
Joan and changed forever after.

THE EXECUTIONER: This still, forbidding figure chills the
scene each time he speaks. He is completely unemotional
though not heartless. But he thinks of himself as a master
craftsman who does his difficult job efficiently. This is far
more terrible than if he were a cruel man who enjoyed causing suffering.

AN ENGLISH SOLDIER: He makes a brief but effective appearance in the Epilogue. He must have led a less than im-
perfect life, for he now dwells in Hell—except for one day a
year, when he is released from torment because he gave a
cross made of two sticks to a girl who was about to be burned

at the stake. He is a philosophical scoundrel; taking things as they come. (He does not find Hell nearly as bad as the French wars.) His one good deed is the only thing he is a little uncomfortable about. He speaks of it defensively, as if he expects to be reproached or laughed at. It is worth noting that he is the last person to desert Joan in the Epilogue—and that only because it is time for him to return to Hell.

ESSAY QUESTIONS AND ANSWERS

1. What are Joan's weaknesses, and how do they contribute to her downfall?

ANSWER: As Shaw portrays her, Joan is a genius. That is, she is a human being at a far more advanced state of mental development than the majority of her fellow men. Her understanding is more profound, and therefore her behavior is more independent and, to ordinary people, more unusual.

The main problem of the genius is to make his insights and actions acceptable to everyday human beings. This Joan fails to do. One reason is her youth. She is executed before she is twenty years old. Thus she does not have time to learn about the less noble kinds of human reactions. She is sure that, if she understands something, those who do not understand it will be grateful to her for making it clear. If others are wrong, she need only tell them what is right. But in fact, ordinary mortals find nothing more unbearable than having their own stupidity or error exposed. This alone is reason enough for most people to hate a genius. As Shaw points out in the Preface to the play, Socrates was tried and executed in ancient Greece for no other crime than this.

Therefore, though Joan is able to attract and influence people temporarily, they soon grow tired of her clear superiority and of the great demands she makes on their own better natures. For instance, the Dauphin is stirred from his laziness and pettiness by Joan's great vision of France as the land of God, held by the King as God's bailiff. But he soon grows weary with doing what he does not really want to. Finally, he just wishes Joan would go home. The Archbishop is another person who is moved by Joan at first and then returns to his own natural behavior.

Also, Joan is naive an unlearned in the ways of the great world. She does not understand the implications of some of her actions. To the end, she cannot understand why the wrath of the Church has been brought down upon her, when she is

a pious girl who obeys the will of God. She says that she understands the will of God better than the Church does. The
Church knows that if it permits such behavior, its downfall
can result.

Again Joan misunderstands when she hopes that her followers
will rescue her from imprisonment. She does not realize that
taking someone from the hands of the Church by force is an
extremely serious matter.

To summarize, Joan is young, tactless, naive, and innocent of
the medieval world. She inspires people, but eventually they
wish she would go away and stop telling them what to do. She
wounds people's pride, thus rousing their hatred. In addition,
she fails to understand the institutions of her own time.

2. What is the relation of the Preface to the play?

ANSWER: The Preface to *Saint Joan* is closely concerned with
the content of the play. Not all of Shaw's prefaces discuss the
subjects of the plays they are supposed to explain. Sometimes
Shaw makes a preface an excuse to discuss some subject that
interests him, referring only incidentally to the play. For instance, the Preface to *Androcles and the Lion,* which is con-
siderably longer than the play itself, is a discussion of the
nature of Christianity. Only occasionally does it refer to the
play. In the case of *Saint Joan,* however, the Preface sticks
to the subject of Joan. It discusses her life, social background,
education, character, peculiarities, weaknesses, and genius. In
connection with this, it also discusses medieval society, especially the Church and the feudal system. It traces the history
of Joan's reputation, including her appearances in literature.
It compares the world of the fifteenth century with the world
of the twentieth century.

In other words, this Preface contains the raw materials of
facts and interpretations out of which the play is made. There
is virtually no action of Joan's or of the others in the play that
is not discussed or clarified somewhere in the Preface.

3. Why are Warwick and Cauchon enemies of Joan?

ANSWER: They are her enemies for obvious political reasons as well as for deeper philosophical reasons. Warwick is an English nobleman whose army has been defeated by Joan and her followers. Cauchon is a bishop who has been ejected from his diocese by Joan's followers.

However, the enmity of the cynical Warwick has a basis in the philosophical ideas that Joan has put forth. Joan feels that a people's natural loyalty is to the king of their country. This loyalty is based on love of the land and a comman tongue. Warwick knows that his strength and that of other great feudal lords like him depends on the loyalty of each man to his feudal superior, without regard to language and place of origin. To Joan, a nation belongs to God. Its king holds it and rules. In the scheme a nobleman has no important place. He becomes an ornamental courtier, nothing more. Thus Warwick is a bitter enemy of Joan's political ideas, which Cauchon has given the name of "Nationalism."

In the same way, Cauchon realizes the dangerous implications in Joan's feelings about God and the Church. Joan feels that her soul answers directly to God. God has commanded her actions. She can do nothing but obey. And though she is a loving daughter of the Church, the commands of God are pre-eminent. She will be faithful to them—to the death if need be. Cauchon visualizes the chaos that could result if any ignorant man or woman could claim to have heard God's direct command. The entire structure of the Church would crumble; it would be a triumph of the devil.

For this reason Cauchon forcefully opposes what he sees as Joan's heresy. He has seen it in other people—in the English reformer Wycliffe and the Bohemian reformer Hus. Warwick names this heresy for him; he calls it "Protestantism." Though Cauchon has pity for the young Maid personally he gives no quarter to her Protestantism.

Of course, the real Warwick and Cauchon did not realize so clearly that Joan was a forerunner of nationalism and Protestantism. Their clearsightedness is a dramatic device which Shaw uses to make obvious the currents of thoughts which existed in the fifteenth century.

4. What does the character of Chaplain Stogumber contribute to the play?

ANSWER: Stogumber makes several contributions to the play. He allows Shaw the opportunity to satirize the mental limitations of a certain type of Englishman. He shows by his own reaction the horror of Joan's execution. And he demonstrates how dangerous a man can be who has a lack of imagination.

In most of those scenes where he appears, Stogumber is an Englishman concerned above all for the success of the English cause. It seems to him that it is natural for the English to win battles; this is an idea he never examines or questions. If the English are losing, there is something abnormal going on. Joan defeats them, so Joan must be a witch. He hates her with a deep hatred as a result. Shaw amusingly portrays here the type of Englishman who assumes with irritating certainty the superiority of the English over everybody else, a type of person not uncommon in Shaw's lifetime.

One of the most powerful moments in the play occurs near the end, when Stogumber, who has done everything to speed Joan's burning except light the fire with his own hands, enters in hysteria. He has seen the real horror of Joan's death with his own eyes. He has been shocked into pity and humanity. By showing the effect of the execution on Stogumber, Shaw impresses us with its soul-shaking dreadfulness. Yet not a touch of violence is ever shown on the stage.

Stogumber's reaction has another purpose as well. It shows us how vicious people can be simply because they do not have the imagination to understand their own cruelty. Stogumber is not a bad man. We see him in the Epilogue as an aged, gentle priest whose mind goes astray at times. He has never been the same since the burning at Rouen. He explains that the sufferings of Jesus Christ were not enough to save him. He did not have imagination enough to comprehend them. For people like him, a new Christ must die in each generation.

5. What is the purpose of the Epilogue?

ANSWER: Shaw points out that Joan's life and death are shown in the play. Joan as a saint is shown in the Epilogue.

The time is 1456, twenty-five years after the trial and death of the Maid. A rather dishonest inquiry has cast aside the verdict of her trial. She is justified as having come from God.

Most important, enough time has passed so that the passionate feelings surrounding Joan's trial and death have cooled. Even Joan herself has a calm about her which is quite different from the turbulence she showed during her lifetime. Now her execution seems far away and not very important. Almost all the important characters in the play reappear during the Epilogue. We see what has happened to each one of them, in twenty-five years; the saint's life has changed some of them and left others untouched.

They learn that Joan will one day become a saint. Each one, in the light of the understanding he has gained with the passing of time, praises the greatness of the Maid. As she accepts these tributes to her glory, Joan observes, "Woe unto me when all men praise me." She offers to come back to life by a miracle. All refuse her offer. Some are sad, some frightened, some horrified at the idea.

The point of this scene is that no real change has taken place in the feelings of ordinary men toward Joan. They praise her now, but than they did when she was alive. The saint glorified is the same as the genius alive and struggling; she is alone. This is perhaps the single most important idea Shaw presents in the play; it is shown with great force and wit in the Epilogue.

CRITICAL COMMENTARY

SAINT JOAN: When *Saint Joan* was produced in 1923, George Bernard Shaw was sixty-seven years of age. He had been a world-famous writer for many years. Just before this, Shaw had offered to the world *Heartbreak House,* a symbolic commentary on Europe before World War I, and *Back to Methuselah,* an incredibly long (five evenings' playing time) philosophical discussion of the history and future of the human race. There was some tendency on the part of playgoers and critics to look upon Shaw as an important literary figure who was growing somewhat long-winded and boring in his old age.

The appearance of *Saint Joan* belied such opinions. The deeply admiring response to this play has continued to our own day. Even in France, where they were suspicious of a play on their warrior saint by a foreigner, the play was received with whole-hearted praise.

Almost all critics who have discussed *Saint Joan* have called it Shaw's finest play. Homer E. Woodbridge, in *G. B. Shaw, Creative Artist,* refers to it as the greatest historical tragedy of the century. C. B. Purdom describes it as tragic in concept, with undertones of comedy; the two elements blend into a perfect unity.

Special notice should be taken of the generous appreciation of the play by the major German novelist Thomas Mann, in an essay written at the time of Shaw's death and included in Louis Kronenberger's collection, *George Bernard Shaw: A Critical Survey.* Mann writes of the fervent tone of the play. He calls it poetically moving. In it, he observes, Shaw's own powerful spirit "bows before sanctity." To Mann, *Saint Joan* fully deserves its enormous fame.

Shaw insists in his Preface that *Saint Joan* is a realistic play, unlike earlier romantic distortions of Joan's life and character. Yet critics (and most readers) have observed that one of the plays most appealing features is Shaw's reverent love of Joan. Purdom, in *A Guide to the Plays of Bernard Shaw*, writes that

Joan's appeal to Shaw was in the way she stood by her conscience against the pressure of authority and was crushed by authority at last. For goodness, truth, and purity make the world uncomfortable, and the world destroys them if it can. Thomas Mann too finds that the rational man in Shaw takes second place here to the worshiper of the saint.

Homer Woodbridge regards the play as having deeper religious values than anything else Shaw ever wrote. Also, it shows a great human being winning a spiritual victory in the midst of worldly disaster. This makes it a tragedy.

Different scenes of the play have their special admirers. Purdom praises the Inquisitor's speech on the nature of heresy as the greatest thing in the play. It is the longest speech in *Saint Joan,* taking about seven minutes to deliver. It explains the reason for the Church's distrust of Joan with magnificent clarity. The most impressive scene, according to Woodbridge, is Stogumber's hysterical return to the scene of Joan's trial after he has witnessed her execution. This frightful reaction of Joan's bitterest enemy gives the emotional impact of Joan's burning as nothing else could.

Any unfavorable criticism the play has received concerns mainly the scenes which contain intellectual analysis. Scene IV, in which Cauchon and Warwick define Nationalism and Protestantism, has occasionally been singled out for such criticism. Thomas Mann writes that the scene might better have been omitted from the play; he suggests that the material in it could have been more suitably discussed in the Preface.

Some critics do not care for the Epilogue. They feel that it is a letdown from the high tragic mood of the trial scene. However, there is no doubt that the Epilogue contains one of the most vital ideas in the play—that geniuses are an embarrassing nuisance to ordinary people.

CRITICAL COMMENTARY: GENERAL REMARKS

There has been a great deal of criticism written about the life, work, and thought of George Bernard Shaw. His career was long; he was exposed to criticism for over half a century during his own lifetime, and since his death in 1950 the commentary has continued. There is almost no drama critic who has not had his chance to write something about Bernard Shaw, for productions of Shaw's plays are unceasing. It is surprising that so little of this criticism is really intelligent or enlightening. It is well known that much criticism of Shaw is weak; Eric Bentley remarks upon this in his valuable short book, *Bernard Shaw*.

What are the reasons for this? Why is the criticism of Shaw less intelligent as a whole than the criticism of Shakespeare, for instance, when Shakespeare is a more puzzling and more intricate writer than Shaw?

One reason may well be Shaw's deceptive simplicity. He tries to write his plays very clearly, and often he even goes on to explain his purposes all over again in prefaces. Therefore, numerous critics of limited ability are very sure that they understand Shaw. But Shaw is not simple, even though he tries to be clear. In the first place, some of his theories are complicated. It is easy to understand them in a general way, but much harder to absorb all the details. Then too, it may be that Shaw could not explain himself completely. Like many great creative artists, he had certain qualities that he was unaware of himself. Thus, though he could explain what he meant to do, he could not always explain what he actually did do.

A second factor is the anger Shaw arouses in many critics. They are troubled by his ideas and resentful of his self-confident and stinging expression of them. Anger and prejudice do not make a good basis for objective study. (Indeed, it is to be hoped that students will be the superiors of their elders in this. If Bernard Shaw expresses an opinion contrary to what a student believes, the student should remain calm, keep his mind open, and respect Shaw's opinion even if he cannot agree with it. This will often happen, for nobody accepts everything Shaw says, and some people accept very little of it. Above all, he should not fail to appreciate Shaw's writing because he happens to be unsympathetic to some of Shaw's thinking.)

SHAW'S IDEAS: Critical writing about Bernard Shaw usually discusses one or more of the following subjects: his ideas, his talent as a playwright, his writing style, and his life. The reader should try to be aware of any prejudices a critic may have as he reads. This is especially true of discussion about ideas. However, antagonism to Shaw's ideas sometimes affects other discussions, about his plays or his life, for instance.

Shaw's thinking is radical. His ideas on religion, sex, marriage, government, and money are therefore likely to startle or offend people who hold conservative views on any of these subjects. For example, St. John Ervine, an Irish playwright and a friend of Shaw, spends a great deal of space in his biography of Shaw (*Bernard Shaw: His Life, Work and Friends*) explaining why Shaw's socialism is wrong. He is especially concerned with the sameness and regimentation that socialism might create if it were to replace the capitalist economic system. He distrusts the mass of humanity. He is least friendly to those plays which have a political or economic subjects, such as *Major Barbara* and *The Apple Cart*.

Another man who was friendly with Shaw personally but critical of his ideas was Gilbert K. Chesterton. This book, *George Bernard Shaw* (1909), was one of the earliest studies of Shaw and his work, and it is still one of the best, as a result of Chesterton's own fine mind and witty expression. The book combines affectionate appreciation of Shaw's honesty, seriousness, and independence with distress at the way Shaw rejects the usual ideas about sin and guilt; for Chesterton had a deeply religious nature himself and eventually became a Roman Catholic.

Shaw's discussions of sex have always created enemies. In the beginning of his career he was thought too outspoken; an early play, *Mrs. Warren's Profession*, completely broke the rules of censorship and could not be produced. Later the opposite was true. Certain writers who looked upon the sexual impulse as the basis of human behavior were shocked because Shaw felt that certain other parts of life (work, devotion to human betterment) were more important than sex. Among these writers were D. H. Lawrence and Frank Harris. They found him and his work lacking in sexuality and therefore incomplete. The American drama critic George Jean Nathan wrote as essay published in 1931 which lists all the places in his plays where the characters show a distrust or a dislike of sex. This essay is probably the least thoughtful expression of this idea about Shaw's writing. It is reprinted by Louis Kronenberger in *George Bernard Shaw: A Critical Survey*.

There are also segments of Shaw's thought which are regarded by almost everyone as eccentric or wrongheaded. For example, his ideas on medicine seem cranky rather than critical. He does not have very much respect for the idea of germs. He expresses these opinions vividly in the Preface to *Saint Joan*. He is violently opposed to vaccination against smallpox.

Then, too, some of his ideas are easy to make fun of, though on careful consideration there is nothing silly about them. Shaw was a vegetarian. When he was in his forties, his health became poor for a while, and doctors told him it was absolutely necessary to begin eating meat. Shaw refused. He could not bring himself to eat the flesh of slaughtered fellow creatures. He wrote at the time that, if he did die, his funeral procession would consist of oxen, sheep, poultry, and even fish, all mourning the man who would rather die than eat them.

The gentle humor of the passage is touching. Looking back, one must respect the personal habits of a man who lived to be ninety-four years old. But it was easy for a critic who wanted to get an easy laugh in Shaw's lifetime to say that his plays would improve if he ate steak.

We may say, then, that comments on Bernard Shaw as a thinker range from the thoughtfully critical to the crudely hostile. But there are also writers who give a more balanced view of Shaw's ideas. A careful explanation may be found in Eric Bentley's *Bernard Shaw*.

SHAW THE PLAYWRIGHT: Discussion of Shaw as playwright usually concerns his character portrayals. Most commentators agree on the liveliness and wit of the conversation in the plays, but they argue about whether the characters themselves are convincing human beings. Some critics claim that the characters do not have the complexity and warmth of real people. They are only types, or representations of ideas, rather than human beings. Archibald Henderson, the author of the most important biography of Shaw, believes this. He calls Shaw's characters "intellectual abstractions." Other critics feel that, while Shaw's characters are not absolutely realistic, Shaw is able to create a convincing manner of thought and speech for each of them. St. John Ervine says of Shaw's dialogue that it has "the rich tone of an unusual mind and yet is faithful to the nature of the people who speak it."

Homer E. Woodbridge, in *George Bernard Shaw, Creative Artist*, writes of the immense vividness of Shaw's portraits. He says that in Shaw's plays there is a group of unforgettable people who have become a living part of our literary heritage. Joan of Arc is an example.

Some critics have also discussed the structure of Shaw's plays. Shaw himself pointed out in the preface to *Ceasar and Cleopatra* that there is nothing new about the structure of his plays. He tells old stories in familiar ways. Only his ideas make his plays new.

Most critics agree with Shaw's own estimate. But to this they add the comment that even if Shaw's plays are not revolutionary, they are very competently put together. By this they mean that the plays tend to have a beginning, a middle, and an end, and that they move along at a quick pace with many interesting changes of mood and feeling. Only in his last plays did Shaw let his interest in ideas make his plays slow-moving and somewhat disorganized.

A useful study of Shaw with emphasis on dramatic structure

is C. B. Purdom's *A Guide to the Plays of Bernard Shaw*. Purdom analyzes the fine points of structure in the plays.

SHAW'S STYLE: Critical comment on Shaw's writing style is overwhelmingly favorable. A few people do object to the sledgehammer forcefulness with which Shaw pounds home his ideas. One critic says that there are no lyrical (poetic) passages in Shaw's plays. But almost every serious critic in his own way expresses admiration for Shaw's prose, which sounds simple, but which actually is a triumph of economy, clarity, and strength.

Eric Bentley remarks that to understand how much more than "simple" Shaw's writing is, you need only see an ordinary Hollywood movie and a movie of a Shaw play in the same day. The flabbiness and flatness of the first give a clue to the control and force of the second. The modern poet W. H. Auden compares Shaw's writing to the music of Rossini, the great Italian composer of comic opera who wrote *The Barber of Seville*. Shaw has, he says, the same tunefulness, humor, vivacity, and clarity in his words as the master composer has in his music.

SELECTED BIBLIOGRAPHY AND
GUIDE TO FURTHER READING

Many plays by George Bernard Shaw are available in good
paperback editions, such as the Penguin editions. The Modern
Library also has reprinted some of Shaw's plays. There is a
three-volume set of *Selected Plays* published by Dodd, Mead,
and Company. Students should make sure that they secure
a complete copy of a play; if there is a preface, it should be
included. The following plays are of great interest:

Shaw's historical plays:
The Devil's Disciple (1897)
Caesar and Cleopatra (1898)
Androcles and the Lion (1911)

For Shaw's discussion of the nature of love and the relationship
between men and women:
Arms and the Man (1894)
Candida (1894)
Captain Brassbound's Conversion (1899)
Man and Superman (1901-1903)

For Shaw's theories about socialism:
Widowers' Houses (1892)
Mrs. Warren's Profession (1893)
Major Barbara (1905)

About Ireland:
John Bull's Other Island (1904)

About doctors and medicine:
The Doctor's Dilemma (1906)

Shaw's music criticism has been edited by Eric Bentley and
published by Doubleday Anchor Books as a paperback under
the title *Shaw on Music*. His drama criticism is reprinted as
Dramatic Opinions and *Our Theatre in the Nineties* (complete). A later edition edited by A. C. Ward is called *Plays
and Players*. His early critical work on behalf of Ibsen and

his theater, *The Quintessence of Ibsenism*, is also available in paperback.

BOOKS ABOUT SHAW

BIOGRAPHY

Ervine, St. John, *Bernard Shaw: His Life, Work and Friends*, New York: William Morrow and Company, 1956. The author, an Irish playwright and friend of Shaw, is sympathetic to Shaw as a person but criticizes his ideas at great length. The personal details about Shaw's life are much more interesting than the criticism.

Henderson, Archibald, *George Bernard Shaw: Man of the Century*, New York: Appleton-Century-Crofts, 1956. The most complete biography of Shaw.

Pearson, Hesketh, *G. B. S., A Full-Length Portrait*, New York and London: Harper and Brothers, 1942. Contains an excellent selection from Shaw's correspondence.

CRITICAL STUDIES

Bentley, Eric, *Bernard Shaw, 1856-1950*, Norfolk, Conn. New Directions 1947, revised 1957. Valuable especially for Bentley's careful explanation of Shaw's ideas.

Kronenberger, Louis (editor), *George Bernard Shaw: A Critical Survey*, Cleveland and New York: World Publishing Company, 1953. A wide selection of essays on Shaw, covering many aspects of his life and work.

MacCarthy, Desmond, *Shaw*, London: Macgibbon and Kee, 1951. The author, one of the foremost drama critics of his day, here puts together the reviews and discussions of Shaw's plays which he wrote during his long career.

Meisel, Martin, *Shaw and the Nineteenth Century Theater*, Princeton: Princeton University Press, 1963. A study tracing the relationship between Shaw's plays and the conventional stage plays of his time.

Nethercot, Arthur H., *Men and Supermen: The Shavian Portrait Gallery*, Cambridge: Harvard University Press, 1954. Analysis of Shaw's characters.

Purdom, C. B., *A Guide to the Plays of Bernard Shaw*, London: Methuen and Company, 1963. A discussion of the structure, characters, and production of each play.

Woodbridge, Homer E., *George Bernard Shaw, Creative Artist*, Carbondale: Southern Illinois University Press, 1963. A study which evaluates Shaw as a poor thinker but a great playwright.

SHAW ANTHOLOGIES

Wilson, Edwin (editor), *Shaw on Shakespeare*, New York; E. P. Dutton and Company, 1961. A collection of Shaw's comments on Shakespeare, including the reviews of Shakespeare's plays he wrote while a drama critic.

Winsten, Stephen (editor), *The Quintessence of G. B. S.*, New York: Creative Age Press, 1949. A collection of various comments from Shaw's plays, prefaces, and essays arranged according to subject. Pleasant to browse in.

BOOKS ABOUT JOAN OF ARC

The account of Joan's trial Shaw used was the one assembled in five volumes by Jules Quicherat (1841-1849).

Anderson, Maxwell, *Joan of Lorraine.*
Anouilh, Jean, *The Lark.*

See also the Preface to *Saint Joan,* especially the section called "The Maid in Literature." See Comment on this section, above, for detailed discussion of the works Shaw mentions.

NOTES

NOTES

NOTES

NOTES

NOTES

NOTES

NOTES

MONARCH® CRITIQUES OF LITERATURE

Size 5¼"x8½" $2.50—$4.95 Each

8672-8	HEMINGWAY—For Whom the Bell Tolls	8680-1 JAMES—Turn of the Screw & Daisy Miller	8854-2 MODERN AMERICAN DRAMA ($4.95)
8673-6	HEMINGWAY—The Old Man and the Sea	8846-8 JAMES—Washington Square	8624-9 MODERN BRITISH AND IRISH DRAMA
8839-3	HEMINGWAY—Snows of Kilimanjaro	8563-9 JOYCE—Portrait of the Artist as a Young Man & Dubliners	8533-2 MODERN ECONOMISTS (George, Keynes, Hayek, Schumpeter, Galbraith and others)

8672-8 HEMINGWAY—For Whom the Bell Tolls
8673-6 HEMINGWAY—The Old Man and the Sea
8839-3 HEMINGWAY—Snows of Kilimanjaro
8674-4 HEMINGWAY—The Sun Also Rises
8503-5 HERODOTUS—The Persian Wars
8840-1 HERSEY—Bell for Adano, Hiroshima and other works
8841-9 HEYERDAHL—Kon-Tiki and Aku-Aku
8842-7 HILTON—Goodbye, Mr. Chips and Lost Horizon
8896-3 HITLER—Concise Biography
8501-9 HOMER—Iliad
8502-7 HOMER—Odyssey
8784-1 HOPKINS—The Poems

8680-1 JAMES—Turn of the Screw & Daisy Miller
8846-8 JAMES—Washington Square
8563-9 JOYCE—Portrait of the Artist as a Young Man & Dubliners
8564-7 JOYCE—Ulysses

8847-6 KAFKA—The Trial, The Castle and other works
8530-8 KANT—The Philosophy
8785-8 KEATS—The Poems
8715-5 KIPLING—Captains Courageous & other works
8848-4 KIPLING—Kim and The Jungle Books
8889-8 KNOWLES—A Separate Peace
8849-2 KOESTLER—Darkness at Noon

8716-3 LAWRENCE—Sons and Lovers & other works
8681-9 LEE—To Kill a Mockingbird
8682-7 LEWIS—Arrowsmith
8683-5 LEWIS—Babbitt
8684-3 LEWIS—Main Street
8531-6 LOCKE AND HOBBES— The Philosophies
8850-6 LOGIC—Deductive ($3.50)
8685-0 LONDON—Call of the Wild
8786-6 LONGFELLOW—Evangeline & other poems

8564-4 MACHIAVELLI—The Prince
8566-2 MANN—The Major Works
8717-1 MARLOWE—Dr. Faustus and other works
8544-9 MARXIST & UTOPIAN SOCIALISTS (Marx, Engels, Owen, Lenin, & others)
8851-8 MAUGHAM—Moon and Sixpence and Razor's Edge
8622-3 MAUGHAM—Of Human Bondage
8686-8 MELVILLE—Billy Budd
8623-1 MELVILLE—Moby Dick and other works
8852-6 MEREDITH—The Ordeal of Richard Feverel
8532-4 MILL, BENTHAM AND THE UTILITARIAN SCHOOL
8687-6 MILLER—The Crucible and View From the Bridge
8688-4 MILLER—Death of a Salesman
8513-4 MILTON—Paradise Lost and other works
8787-4 MILTON—The Poems (exclusive of Paradise Lost)

8854-2 MODERN AMERICAN DRAMA ($4.95)
8624-9 MODERN BRITISH AND IRISH DRAMA
8533-2 MODERN ECONOMISTS (George, Keynes, Hayek, Schumpeter, Galbraith and others)
8567-0 MODERN EUROPEAN DRAMA
8568-8 MOLIERE—The Plays
8855-9 MONTAIGNE—Essays of
8856-7 MORE—Utopia
8895-5 MUSSOLINI—Concise Biography
8523-3 MYTHOLOGY

8625-6 NEW TESTAMENT ($3.50)
8534-0 NIETZSCHE—The Major Works
8535-7 NINETEENTH-CENTURY SOCIOLOGISTS (Durkheim, Comte, Spencer, Weber and others)
8857-5 NORDHOFF & HALL— Mutiny on the Bounty
8891-4 NORRIS—The Octopus

8626-4 OLD TESTAMENT ($3.50)
8627-2 O'NEILL—The Major Plays
8750-2 O'NEILL—Desire Under the Elms
8751-0 O'NEILL—Iceman Cometh
8752-8 O'NEILL—Long Day's Journey into Night
8753-6 O'NEILL—Mourning Becomes Electra
8754-4 O'NEILL—Strange Interlude
8718-9 ORWELL—Animal Farm
8719-7 ORWELL—1984

8885-6 HOW TO ANALYZE DRAMA ($3.50)
8886-4 HOW TO ANALYZE FICTION ($3.50)
8887-2 HOW TO ANALYZE POETRY ($3.50)
8834-4 HOW TO WRITE THEMES ($3.50)
8888-0 HOW TO WRITE THESES ($3.50)
8675-1 HOWELLS—Rise of Silas Lapham
8844-3 HUGO—Les Miserables
8529-0 HUME—The Philosophy
8714-8 HUXLEY—The Major Novels (Brave New World, Point Counterpoint and others)
8562-1 IBSEN—The Major Plays
8676-9 IRVING—Legend of Sleepy Hollow
8677-7 JAMES—The Ambassadors
8678-5 JAMES—The American
8845-0 JAMES—The Aspern Papers
8629-3 JAMES—Portrait of a Lady

GREAT IDEA SERIES
SERIES SHOWN HERE FOR REFERENCE ONLY.
TITLES IN ALPHABETICAL LISTS ABOVE AND ON OTHER PAGES

Philosophers and Political Philosophers

AMERICAN POLITICAL PHILOSOPHY
ARISTOTLE—The Philosophy ($3.50)
BERKELEY—The Philosophy
COMMUNIST THEORY FROM MARX TO MAO, OUTLINE & CRITICISM OF ($3.50)
CONSTITUTION—Leading Cases ($3.50)
DARWIN AND SPENCER
DESCARTES—The Philosophy
EARLY CHURCH FATHERS— The Writings ($3.50)
FEDERALIST PAPERS
FREUD—On His Writings and Ideas
HEGEL—The Philosophy
HUME—The Philosophy
KANT—The Philosophy

LOCKE AND HOBBES— The Philosophies
LOGIC—Deductive ($3.50)
MILL, BENTHAM AND THE UTILITARIAN SCHOOL
NIETZSCHE—The Major Works
PLATO—The Republic and Selected Dialogues
ROUSSEAU AND THE 18TH-CENTURY POLITICAL PHILOSOPHERS
RUSSELL—The Philosophy
ST. THOMAS AQUINAS— The Philosophy
ST. AUGUSTINE—The Works
SCHOPENHAUER—The Philosophy
SCIENCE—The Philosophy of ($4.95)
SPINOZA—The Philosophy
TWENTIETH-CENTURY FASCISM
TWENTIETH-CENTURY PHILOSOPHERS

UNITED NATIONS ($4.95)
VOLTAIRE—Candide (and the Philosophes)

Economists

CLASSICAL ECONOMISTS (Smith, Ricardo and Malthus)
MARXIST & UTOPIAN SOCIALISTS (Marx, Engels, Owen, Lenin, & others)
MODERN ECONOMISTS (George, Keynes, Hayek, Schumpeter, Galbraith & others)

Sociology & Education

NINETEENTH-CENTURY SOCIOLOGISTS (Durkheim, Comte, Spencer, Weber & others)
20TH-CENTURY EDUCATORS
TWENTIETH-CENTURY SOCIOLOGISTS (Lerner, Riesman, and many others)